THE SECRET
HEIRESS

THE SECRET HEIRESS

LILLIAN SHELLEY

DOUBLEDAY & COMPANY, INC.
GARDEN CITY, NEW YORK
1982

All of the characters in this book
are fictitious, and any resemblance
to actual persons, living or dead,
is purely coincidental.

Library of Congress Cataloging in Publication Data

Shelley, Lillian.
The secret heiress.

I. Title.
PS3569.H3933C3   813'.54
AACR2
ISBN 0-385-17836-0
Library of Congress Catalog Card Number 81–43534

First Edition

*To Dorothy Provenzano for her friendship
and to Jeannette Ghaney for her helpful suggestions
and unfailing patience.
A special thanks to Alfred Koppel for
first throwing down the gauntlet.*

THE SECRET
HEIRESS

CHAPTER 1

Caroline Chessington regarded herself in the looking glass.

"No," she said aloud. "Mr. Farrowby quite overstated the case."

Mr. Farrowby, in making his offer to Miss Chessington, had indeed called her a goddess. Miss Chessington, however, was painfully aware that an heiress with £50,000 a year was often subject to such fulsome compliments. She was, moreover, an honest young woman, and she knew herself to be no more than passably good-looking.

It would be nice, she thought, to have a gentleman say to me, I am aware, Miss Chessington, that you are too tall, that your nose is a trifle long, and that your hair is mousy brown. Yet still I desire to marry you because I stand in desperate need of your fortune. At least then he would be honest. Miss Chessington smiled faintly. In fact, Caroline did herself an injustice. Although somewhat taller than fashion decreed, her figure was lithe and well formed. She carried herself with the easy assurance that came of centuries of privilege. The hair she dismissed as mousy brown was in reality a soft chestnut brown. And though her nose could have been a trifle shorter, her wide, intelligent brown eyes, under well-shaped brows, more than made up for this slight defect. Her generally serious demeanor was lightened by a lively wit and a charming smile. No, Caroline Chessington was hardly an antidote.

An only child, born late in the lives of an extremely wealthy baronet and his lady, both now deceased, Caroline Chessington had inherited a large fortune. She lived in Lancashire in the family home, Brampton Hall, with an elderly cousin and the nurse and servants who had been with her since childhood. Her parents had led a quiet life, preferring to remain in the country the year round. Their illness and age had prevented her going to London for her first Season, and somehow, for one reason or another, Caroline had never gone. Now, at twenty-seven, she rarely left her own district, save for a journey in the summer to the seaside at Morecambe.

While many young women might have considered such a life little more than a prison sentence, it suited Miss Chessington very well. She enjoyed being mistress of the household, and took an active interest in the management of her considerable estate. Brampton had always been a working farm. Caroline had become interested in the new agricultural methods that were gaining acceptance in England, and she was engaged in a lengthy, continuing correspondence with Mr. Coke of Holkham and Arthur Young, who had been Secretary of Agriculture. Initial reactions of surprise at her interest were followed by letters of encouragement and suggestions. Mr. Young, indeed, regretted that his great age prevented him from traveling to Brampton to meet Caroline.

Moreover, Caroline loved the Hall itself and its extensive gardens. Brampton Hall was one of the oldest houses in the neighborhood; records kept in the muniment room showed references to the manor in the Domesday Book and in other historical documents. The main building was a particularly fine example of a Tudor half-timbered manor house in the style common to Lancashire and was well known for its rich linenfold paneling and plaster work. Subsequent centuries had seen many changes as succeeding heirs had added what was currently fashionable. The mixture of architectural styles was one of the reasons that the building held such charm for Caroline. One of her great pleasures was to walk the length of the gallery where the ancestral portraits were hung. Her sense of family pride was heightened by looking at the portraits of past generations of Chessingtons dressed in the various costumes of previous times.

Caroline never lacked for social activity, either. She visited regularly with neighbors and had several close friends and acquaintances among the local gentry. Brampton, the market village for the area, hosted a monthly Assembly. Caroline, an acknowledged leader in the district, enjoyed the balls for the dancing. If the same company, known from childhood, was sometimes a trifle flat, it had the comfortable feeling of the familiar. Any feelings of restiveness or discontent were shrugged off with the practical notion of how much there was to occupy her at Brampton.

Nor had Caroline lacked suitors, though it had not taken her long to realize that few of the gentlemen who sought her out would have had the least interest in her if she were separated from her money. That knowledge had made her wary of meeting new people; she preferred to trust those friends who she knew valued her. Her cousin, Aurelia, had often remonstrated at the ordered life she led, suggesting to Caroline that she go to London.

"For you know, my love," she would say, "that I am not thinking of myself. No indeed. If I had my choice, I should never leave our own delightful, snug home! But you—surely you must long for a sight of London. To go to parties and Assemblies! To dance at Almack's! And," she would continue in the arch manner which she affected, "to meet so many more eligible young gentlemen than you can meet here. Surely you must wish for that."

No, thought Caroline. She certainly did not wish to go to London. As soon as it became known that she was in possession of a large fortune, every gazetted fortune hunter in London would be at her door. In London there were probably dozens of Mr. Farrowbys.

There was a knock on the door.

"Come in," said Caroline. It was Sarah, her personal maid.

"Miss Caroline, Preston says to tell you that Lady Skipton and

Miss Skipton have come to call. He's put them in the morning room."

"Thank you, Sarah," said Caroline. "Please tell Preston I shall be there directly and ask him to bring Lady Skipton and Miss Skipton some refreshments."

"Yes, Miss Caroline," said Sarah. She dropped a little curtsy as she left.

"Oh, dear," said Caroline when she was alone. "No doubt they've already learned of Mr. Farrowby's visit and have come to find out if it is indeed true that I am prepared to throw away another chance at marriage. Still, I guess I had better see them before the entire village is talking of it." She patted her hair into place and prepared to greet her visitors.

The morning room in which Lady Skipton and her daughter, Sophronia, were seated, was one of the more comfortable rooms in the house. Its diamond-pane windows looked out on a broad expanse of lawn edged with masses of rhododendrons. This part of the house had been added some two hundred years before, to provide more private and less drafty accommodations than the older Great Hall and parlor allowed.

Caroline's visitors had indeed come to find out what they could. Lady Skipton, a short, rather plump woman and Caroline's closest neighbor, had long ago appointed herself guardian of her welfare. Her daughter Sophronia, already safely betrothed to a respectable country gentleman, was a number of years younger than Caroline and stood somewhat in awe of her competent and self-sufficient neighbor.

"Mama," Sophronia said rather tentatively, while they were waiting, "perhaps Miss Chessington will not like to have us inquiring about Mr. Farrowby."

"Nonsense, Sophronia," said her mother, dismissing such an idea. "I am certain that Caroline realizes that my interest is not vulgar curiosity, but a genuine concern for her future. As she has no mother, it is no less than my duty."

"Yes, Mama," said Sophronia. She said no more because, at that moment, Caroline entered the room. She was wearing the same pink sprigged-muslin dress in which she had greeted Mr. Farrowby.

"How do you do, Lady Skipton," she said. "And Sophronia, how nice to see you."

"Hello, Caroline," said Lady Skipton. "I am pleased to see that you have taken my advice and have begun wearing colors which do not emphasize your sallow complexion."

"Mama!" bleated Sophronia.

"Caroline knows that I do not stand on ceremony with her but regard her as if she were my daughter."

"Yes, indeed, ma'am," said Caroline, maintaining her composure, for she knew that all four of Lady Skipton's daughters were intimidated by their redoubtable parent.

"And I am certain," continued Lady Skipton, "that Caroline knows my interest in Mr. Farrowby's visit is only because I wish to see her happily established, as her own mother would have wished."

"I thank you very much for your concern, Lady Skipton," said Caroline. "However, I am afraid that you have made this trip in vain. I do not intend to marry Mr. Farrowby. He and I should not at all suit."

"I believe you to be a sensible young woman, Caroline," began Lady Skipton. "However, you cannot intend to continue to remain unmarried, living here with only your cousin and servants for protection."

"Protection, ma'am? In Brampton? From what should I stand in need of protection?"

"You know very well, Caroline, that I refer to the protection of a man's name and of his wise counsel; someone to take charge of the management of your fortune."

"Since I have come of age, ma'am, I have had control of my fortune, with the wise counsel of my man of business. I do not think I have managed ill. That there are many gentlemen desirous of taking charge of the management of my affairs I am well aware. Indeed, many of them would prefer that I not go along with it!"

There was a titter from Sophronia's direction, quelled quickly by a glance from her mother.

"To be sure, Caroline, a young woman in your position is prey to the fortune hunter. All the more reason for you to ally yourself with a gentleman who can protect you from them."

"Such as Mr. Farrowby, ma'am?"

"Mr. Farrowby is a gentleman of good breeding. When you were younger, a woman with your fortune could have hoped for a title. Now, and I do not mince words, Caroline, Mr. Farrowby would be an excellent choice!"

"Mr. Farrowby and I share no common interests. I have no reason to believe that he feels any more for me than I feel for him."

"I am certain, Caroline, that your dear mother would be shocked to hear you speak so! You speak as if you were a merchant's daughter! That is what comes of being so long on your own and so involved in matters so foreign to female sensibilities. I cannot think what is to be done if you continue to refuse such eligible suitors as Mr. Farrowby!"

"I hope, ma'am, that I shall continue on as comfortably as I have in the past."

"If only you had gone to London for your presentation," said Lady Skipton, ignoring Caroline's last remarks. "As soon as it were known that you were an heiress—and of good family, as well—you would have had the opportunity to make a good match."

"Then I must say, Lady Skipton, that I am glad I have not gone to London! I begin to feel like one of my sheep being sold to the highest bidder!"

"I can see, my dear Caroline, that your nerves are overset. I have long felt that dealing with business best left to men would prove too much. You talk as though being a considerable heiress were a hindrance, not an advantage. I do not scruple to tell you that for a young woman who is by no means a great beauty, a sizable dowry is of the utmost importance. You might as well go to London incognita, so that no one will know you are an heiress. I have never known you to be so foolish! Sophronia, yes, but you, no!"

Caroline could not help laughing. "I am sorry, ma'am, to be such a disappointment to you. I know you are concerned about me and I do thank you for it, but truly, there is no need to worry. We go on quite well as we are, and I am quite capable of managing my affairs. I would much rather hear about Sophronia's wedding plans. I am certain you must be so busy!"

Lady Skipton, recognizing the stubborn tone in Caroline's voice, turned to Sophronia, who blushed at becoming the focus of attention. She began talking about her gowns, and the three women were soon involved in a discussion of fashion, in which the merits of various fabrics and styles were debated. She had brought the latest copy of *La Belle Assemblée* and shyly showed Caroline the sketches of several costumes which she wished to have. Lady Skipton pointed out how fortunate it was that Paris fashions were again available now that the war with the monster Napoleon was indeed over. The Skiptons remained for a short time, partaking of the offered refreshments. Caroline did not give Lady Skipton further opportunity to return to the subject of her visit, and when they departed, Lady Skipton remarked that she would speak to Caroline alone at another time.

"I should hope not," said Caroline wearily to herself when they were safely out of earshot. "I am quite bored with the subject of my future."

"Did you say something, my love?" asked Cousin Aurelia, coming into the room.

"No, I was just thinking aloud," replied Caroline.

"Was that Lady Skipton's carriage I saw? You should have called me. Had I known they had come to call, I would have come to greet them, though I was resting in my room. I hope she did not consider my absence a slight."

"I am certain she did not," said Caroline. "Lady Skipton came particularly to speak to me."

"I wonder what for," said Aurelia. "Perhaps she wished to speak of Sophronia's wedding."

"We did speak of the wedding," said Caroline, wishing to avoid a further discussion of Mr. Farrowby. "Sophronia accompanied her."

"Such a lovely thing, a wedding," said Aurelia. "I remember when my own dear sister was married to Mr. Bensonhurst. Such fun we had: the gowns, the shoes, the hats! Of course, we were not wealthy, though dear Papa had provided for us as best he could. And I remember the wedding of your own dear parents. Such a lovely bride your mother was. And now, of course," she concluded coyly, "we look forward to your wedding, dear Caroline."

Caroline had heard quite enough for one day about plans for her marriage. With a great deal of effort, she held her temper and said merely, "How eager everyone is to see me married! I shall begin to think you are all trying to be rid of me. Let us hear no more about my wedding. And now, please excuse me. I must speak to Keith about the new garden." She strode out of the room.

"Well!" said Cousin Aurelia after her. "I wonder what I said!"

Caroline's sense of humor made it impossible for her not to see the ridiculous aspects of the situation. As a restorative measure, she took a few turns around the gardens, a particularly favorite place since they had been laid out by her father. She then sought out Keith, the head gardener, for consultation about some cut flowers for the house. His calm, laconic disposition restored her temper. She knew, however, that neither Lady Skipton nor

Cousin Aurelia were likely to leave the matter where it now stood. They might accept the fact that she would not marry Mr. Farrowby, but they would not cease trying to find her a husband. If they could not find one here, they would persist in trying to persuade her to go to London. She thought of Lady Skipton's remark about her going to London incognita, and she smiled. "At least then I should know that the gentlemen who offer for me like me for my nose as well as for my fortune!"

She stopped. Was it such an outrageous idea? She had never been to London and was not known there. What family she had was not in London. She could take a house in a quiet, genteel neighborhood; not a fashionable district, but a solid and respectable one. She would have no difficulty in persuading Cousin Aurelia, or her old nurse, Mrs. Lawson, to accompany her, but she knew they would not approve of her desire to hide her identity. She could fashion a story to give out to people she met; that would be easy compared to the resistance she would have to overcome at home. It could be done, and it would be a welcome diversion. She would have to think about it. It was an idea worth pursuing.

CHAPTER 2

When Caroline came downstairs for dinner, she greeted Cousin Aurelia with a smile. Caroline genuinely pitied the older woman's position; having had money all her life, she could only imagine the difficulty of being dependent on relations for one's comfort. She also knew that she could not go to London without a companion, and that it would be foolish to antagonize her cousin.

"I see Keith has brought some flowers from the greenhouse," she said, admiring the cut blossoms in a vase on the sideboard. "Aren't they lovely?"

"I have often thought that the gardens and greenhouses here at Brampton are the loveliest and best in the county," said Cousin Aurelia. "They are a tribute to your skill, my dear Caroline."

"Oh, indeed not," said Caroline. "I don't know what I would do without Keith! I merely make suggestions; his is the talent that makes them work." She hastened to change the subject, never being comfortable with the excessive compliments her cousin felt were necessary.

"Have you finished the volume of Lord Byron's latest poems?" asked Caroline, seeking a safe topic.

"Ah, Lord Byron," sighed Aurelia. "Such a handsome young man and such beautiful verses. If I were younger, I would be in danger of losing my heart. But you, my dear Caroline, I believe, are not an admirer?"

"I must admit that I prefer the works of Miss Austen, but I know that in not greatly admiring Lord Byron both for his verses and his face I have been in the minority. But Aurelia, surely you do not admire his treatment of his wife and child. And now he has left England under such questionable circumstances . . ."

"Ah, so unfortunate," answered Aurelia, adding, "the latest *on dit* is even more scandalous than his escapades with Lady Caroline Lamb. To think they involve his sister!" She broke off, embarrassed.

At that moment the main courses were served and the ladies devoted themselves to the ham and turbot embellished with various side dishes which were set before them. Cousin Aurelia, whose appetite, despite her gaunt and bony appearance, was hearty, ate all that was served her.

"My dear Caroline, you are barely touching the ham," she remarked. "Is it not to your liking?"

"I don't seem to be very hungry tonight," she replied. "I am a bit preoccupied."

"May one ask what is on your mind?" asked Aurelia in the arch tone which Caroline disliked. "Or is it a private matter?"

"No, it is not at all private," said Caroline. "In fact, it involves you. I am thinking of taking a house in London for the Season."

"In London! My dear Caroline!" exclaimed her cousin. "You must know that I have hoped you would do so for such a long time! You must take a house in Mount Street or one of the other very fashionable locations. It is of the utmost importance that you establish yourself in the first stare of elegance. Once it is known that you are of good family and an heiress as well, it will not be long before you are, as they say, 'all the rage.' Oh, there is so much to do before we leave!"

Caroline listened patiently until Aurelia was finished. She studied her hands for a moment before speaking.

"It is not my intention to seek lodgings in the most fashionable location," she said. "I would like to find a house in a quiet, genteel district."

"A quiet, genteel district!" exclaimed Aurelia. "You must be funning, my love. Such a move would be fatal. You would be marked as a provincial with no *ton*."

"Cousin Aurelia, I am a provincial. I have no desire to make my mark in Society. I go to London to see London. I am eager to see the Houses of Parliament and the Elgin Marbles and other objects of interest."

"The Elgin Marbles! But they are in the British Museum! You cannot mean to go to museums and such in London! No matter how great an heiress you are, you cannot wish to be known as a bluestocking. Even the wealthy Miss Chessington could not survive such a reputation."

"Then you may put your mind at rest, Aurelia," said Caroline. "No one will even know that I am Miss Chessington. I intend to go under a different name; perhaps Chessley or something of the like. It must not be too dissimilar or I shall forget to answer to it."

"Caroline!" shrieked Aurelia. "You cannot mean that! Oh, my word, what is to be done? If only your poor parents were here! Why would you do such a vulgar thing? If it became known, you would be an outcast! No one would receive you. And why? Pray, tell me why?" She brought her vinaigrette, never far from her side, to her nose as she moaned.

"Please calm yourself, Aurelia. I do not mean to distress you, but I do not intend to go to London to put myself on the block or to sell myself to the highest bidder." There was another moan. "If I go under an assumed name, no one will be aware of my fortune. If I meet someone who cares for me without my fortune, he shall certainly care for me with it."

"Only think, Caroline," pleaded Aurelia desperately. "Only think of the scandal if it became known that you had done such a thing. An assumed name! Only a very vulgar sort of person would use an assumed name, I am certain."

"Perhaps an assumed name is not necessary," conceded Caroline. "After all, my parents never went to London and I have no family there. No doubt Miss Chessington would mean nothing in London. It would be confusing to have to answer to another name. All right, Aurelia, I shall go as Miss Chessington."

"Oh, my dear Caroline . . ."

"But," continued Caroline, "I do intend to live in a quiet district and keep my wealth a secret. I shall depend on you and Mrs. Lawson to keep my secret. Will you help me?"

Aurelia's hand fluttered helplessly. "I do not know what to say. To pretend is unlike anything I have ever done."

"If you feel that you cannot, Aurelia, I shall have to go to London with only Mrs. Lawson to bear me company."

That finished it. Aurelia was extremely jealous of Caroline's old nurse and the influence she had. She also knew that Caroline, once her mind was set, was quite capable of carrying out her plan. Despite Caroline's disclaimers about entering into London Society, Aurelia certainly did not wish to miss the trip to London. And finally, she was dependent on Caroline for her present standard of living. The economies which would be necessary if she had to exist on her own were too unpleasant to contemplate. She would have to go to London on Caroline's terms.

"Very well, Caroline," she said with a sniff. "We shall go to London as you wish."

"You must promise, Aurelia, that you will not let slip the fact that I am an heiress."

"You may be sure that I am able to keep a secret," said Aurelia with another sniff.

"Indeed!" said Caroline, getting up and going over to kiss her cousin's cheek. "You'll see; we'll have a lovely time, and we shall go to the theater and the opera. I must write to Stokes, my man of business, you know, and ask him to engage a house for us. And, of course, I must speak to Mrs. Lawson. I am certain that she will raise at least as many objections as you have!"

"If I am willing to accompany you, I see no reason why a servant should question the decision," said Aurelia.

"Then you don't know her very well," said Caroline.

The next morning, Caroline sought out Mrs. Lawson in her quarters. A tall woman with an ample bosom and a comfortable look, she had been Caroline's nurse as a child and still considered Caroline her personal province. She scolded Caroline as if she were still a child if she came in damp after a ride, cosseted her with potions if she caught a cold, and allowed no one else the honor of sewing her darling's ripped hems. She considered Cousin Aurelia a poor companion for her pet. She lived for the day when Caroline would marry (although she doubted there was anyone worthy of her) and set up her own nursery, where Mrs. Lawson fully intended to hold sway. When Caroline knocked on her door, she was working on the linens which were her contribution to Caroline's trousseau, and on which she had been working for years.

"Why, Miss Caroline!" she exclaimed as she looked up from her work. "And what might you be doing here?"

"Hello, Awson-Lawson," she said, using her childhood pet name for the nurse.

"Now, go on then, Miss Caroline," said Mrs. Lawson with a pleased smile. "When you were a little girl you used to call me that when you were wanting something or had done something wrong. Now which is it?"

"How well you know me, dear Nurse," said Caroline with a laugh. "I haven't done anything wrong yet, so don't glower at me! I am planning to take a house in London and hope you will come with me."

"As if I'd be letting you go alone, Miss Caroline," scolded Mrs. Lawson. "You as has never been outside of Lancashire. And who else would be taking care of you, I'd like to know?"

"It certainly would not seem right if it were not my oldest friend," said Caroline. "I shall depend on you."

"And when might you be planning to go, Miss Caroline?"

asked Mrs. Lawson. "There's much that needs doing before we're ready."

"Of course, I shall have to arrange for a house in London. Once that is done, it only awaits our preparations here. There is one thing."

"And what's that, Miss Caroline?" asked the nurse.

Knowing well that the knowledge that Cousin Aurelia was against something was the surest way to win Mrs. Lawson over to her side, Caroline said, "My cousin believes I should hire a house in the most fashionable part of town, announcing that I am an heiress. I should prefer to live more quietly, keeping my wealth a secret. You know how much I dislike being toadeaten because I am wealthy!"

"Indeed I do, Miss Caroline. Many's the time I've said to myself it's a shame, the way some people as I won't mention, toady to you and bother you until you don't know which end's up. Un-Christian, that's what I call it."

"So you do understand my desire, despite my cousin's feelings, to go as plain, unassuming Miss Chessington?"

"Of course, Miss Caroline, if that's what suits you, then that's what you should do. I'm sure certain people will do just as you say if they know what's good for them." She sniffed.

"Dear Lawson, you're always protecting me, aren't you?"

"I'm sure I know my duty, Miss Caroline, as if caring for you were a duty, which I'm sure it's not. And maybe if we go to London, you'll be able to use these linens I'm making."

Caroline jumped up and kissed her soundly on the cheek. "Thank you so much, Lawson," she said. "I don't know what I'd do without you."

"Hmph," said Lawson. But Caroline had no doubt that she was pleased.

Back in her room, Caroline sat down to consider the situation. She was a bit weary from the placating of the two old adversaries, but now that she had overcome this obstacle, the difficult part of the scheme seemed behind her.

"Now I reckon I must write to Stokes and ask him to find a suitable house," she said. "I certainly hope that when he learns of my plans, he will not also raise objections to the location. I don't feel capable of handling another elderly protector!"

She went to her writing table, which had been her mother's, and for which she had a special fondness. It was lacquered with flowers and fantastic birds, and was in the popular Chinese style. She took out her writing paper and began composing a letter to Mr. Stokes.

Dear Mr. Stokes:

It is my intention to remove to London for several months, preferably from April to July. I wish to hire a furnished house, with servants, in a quiet, genteel district, one which is not in the most fashionable area.

In addition, as I do not intend to be presented as an heiress, I would appreciate it if you would not reveal my situation to anyone.

Please let me know at your earliest convenience the result of your inquiries.

Very truly yours,
Caroline Chessington

And if that does not surprise the sedate and stolid Mr. Stokes, nothing will, she thought with a grin.

CHAPTER 3

In London, Mr. Stokes had just received the letter from his wealthy client. The Stokes family firm had handled the business affairs of the Chessingtons for several generations. Mr. Stokes had been horrified, six years previously, when Caroline had come of age unmarried. He was particularly distressed at her insistence on taking control of her estate from her trustees, capable men who could be depended upon not to squander it away. However, Caroline had been prudent; holding household, permitting him to invest in the Funds, and showing a shrewder head for business than he had thought possible in a female. He had never had reason to ponder the motives behind one of her requests before, and this letter puzzled him. Mr. Stokes put on his wire-rimmed glasses again and called in his assistant, John Potts.

"Yes, Mr. Stokes?" asked that respectful young gentleman.

"Potts, what do you make of this?" He read Caroline's letter aloud.

"Why, Mr. Stokes, it sounds as if Miss Chessington means to come to London."

"I can see that, you fool. What I don't understand is why she wants a house in an unfashionable district, and why she doesn't want anyone to know she's an heiress. One would suppose she would want every eligible gentleman to know her situation. She is no longer a young woman, you know."

"Perhaps she does not want to be hounded by fortune hunters," suggested Mr. Potts diffidently.

"I don't know why I keep you on," said Mr. Stokes. "A bigger fool I've never known. An unmarried woman of great wealth and no particular beauty not announce her wealth because she fears fortune hunters? How else does she expect to find a husband, if they do not know she is an heiress?"

"When you sent me to Brampton Hall to deliver some papers last year and I met Miss Chessington, I thought her not at all unattractive," said poor Mr. Potts, almost to himself. "She had a very friendly smile and fine eyes."

"Perhaps you'd care to offer for her yourself," said Mr. Stokes with awful irony. "You had better marry money. You are such a fool, you'll never get on in business."

"Yes, sir," said the unhappy Mr. Potts. "And what do you intend to do about the letter, sir?" he asked.

"Do as she asks, of course," said Mr. Stokes. "What else would I do for our wealthiest client? Don't you have some work to do?"

"Yes, sir," said Mr. Potts. He fled.

Miss Chessington was fortunate to hear none of Mr. Stokes's comments on her plans. She waited impatiently for his reply, which was several weeks in coming. It arrived on a rainy March afternoon. Preston brought it into the library, where Caroline was reading, but not really absorbing, a rather boring book and Cousin Aurelia was crocheting a cap for the newborn baby of a distant relation.

"The post, Miss Caroline," said Preston, handing it to her. Like most of the staff, Preston, the head butler, was a local man who had been a family servant since he had started in service as an under-footman. Caroline was a great favorite of the staff, most of whom had been in service at the Hall since before she was born.

"Is there anything of interest, my love?" asked Aurelia.

"There is a letter from my Aunt Horatia in Yorkshire," Caroline said. "It is probably a renewal of her annual invitation to visit her. She will again be relieved when I decline. Ah, here is a letter which appears to be from Mr. Stokes in London. Perhaps he has news of a house for us."

"Oh, I certainly hope so," said Aurelia. "Do, pray, open it quickly."

Caroline opened the letter and read it. "Splendid!" she exclaimed. "Mr. Stokes writes that he has found a house in Woburn Square. He says it is a 'completely respectable, genteel neighborhood, but not one where one would expect to find the *ton!* That sounds perfect! I knew Mr. Stokes could carry out my instructions. He says the owner must let the house for a few months because his wife's ill health forces them to retire to Bath so that she might take the waters. The house is available as soon as we wish it. I believe I shall write to Mr. Stokes and tell him we shall take the house as of the first of April."

"The first of April!" exclaimed Aurelia. "That is only two weeks away, and there is so much to do!"

"But you were saying only yesterday how tiresome it is with the weather so poor. Now we shall have enough to keep us busy until we leave for London. It has been so long since the house was closed for such an extended period that I must speak to the housekeeper about the arrangements that are to be made."

"We must take the best silver and china," said Aurelia, "and the bed linens, for one never knows about the sheets in some of the lesser establishments. And, of course . . ."

"Cousin Aurelia," interrupted Caroline, laughing, "we are going to a perfectly respectable place. I am certain their china and silver is more than adequate and that the servants take excellent care of the linens. And do recollect that we are going to a house in London, not to some local inn. I am certain we shall find everything we might need there. And now I really must speak to Mrs. Sutton, and write to Mr. Stokes with instructions to hire the house." She rushed out of the room without waiting to hear

Aurelia's forebodings about the shortcomings of London's servants.

The household at Brampton was thrown into chaos by the news of the impending journey. The servants, accustomed to a routine which had not varied since Caroline was eighteen, were upset at the news that they would be expected to keep the household running without "Miss Caroline" to turn to. It took the combined efforts of Caroline and Mrs. Lawson to soothe the fears of Cook that Mrs. Sutton would interfere in her kitchen, and to reassure her that they really did not want her to give notice and return to her family. Cousin Aurelia continued issuing orders, to which no one paid heed, because to carry them out would have meant moving the entire household to London.

The day before the journey was to begin, Mrs. Lawson fell down the stairs and broke her leg. This disaster threatened to delay the expedition, but when the doctor informed Caroline that it would be six weeks before Mrs. Lawson would be able to travel, the nurse tearfully implored Caroline to make the trip without her.

"It's not that I don't want to go, Miss Caroline," she said as she wiped her eyes. "But I can't have you spoiling your plans because of me. Stupid it was of me, falling like that. Now you go along to London like you planned. You'll be all right with Miss Peakirk."

Knowing how much that statement had cost Mrs. Lawson, Caroline went to her and kissed her.

"I don't like to leave you," she said.

"Now Miss Caroline, you stop being foolish. There's more than enough servants around here with little enough to do, once you're gone. They can take care of me until I'm up and about."

"You remember that the doctor said you were to stay in bed until your leg is completely healed."

"And just who is the nurse around here?" demanded Mrs. Lawson, beginning to sniffle again. "You have a lot to do, Miss Caroline, and you'd better be running along."

"Yes, ma'am," said Caroline teasingly. She kissed Mrs. Lawson again. As she closed the door behind her, she heard the old woman begin to cry.

There were no further disasters. Finally, the carriages were loaded with baggage and such items as were considered indispensable, at least to Aurelia, and they were on their way. The two-hundred-mile journey from Brampton to London would take several days; Stokes had bespoken the best rooms in the inns where they would stop along the way. At first, Caroline had demurred at Mr. Stokes's insistence on such travel arrangements, but, whatever her intentions for anonymity in London, she had no desire to expose herself or her party to the company of the vulgar persons one might meet at posting inns.

At each stop along the way, a private parlor had been readied for Caroline. Aurelia had insisted on their bringing their own sheets to use at the inns, and at each inn she set the maid to ready Caroline's chamber and the one set aside for herself. At the last night's stop before London, Caroline suggested that they retire early so they could reach London before evening the next day. In fact, she was weary of Aurelia's incessant chatter and was eager for some quiet moments by herself before going to bed.

"Do be careful to bolt the door, my love," admonished Aurelia as she had each night of the journey. "In a public place such as this, one cannot be too careful."

"As we have bespoken the most private parts of these inns and have outriders with us who, we can be certain, will arise at the first cry from us, I do not feel there is any need to worry, Aurelia. This is, after all, the nineteenth century. I am quite certain that we are perfectly safe. Now, good night." She picked up her candle and left for her bedchamber without waiting for a response. The bed, with a bedwarmer having been slid between the sheets to ward off the cold, was inviting, and Caroline was more tired from the journey than she realized. She dismissed Sarah and it was not long before she was asleep.

The next morning Caroline awakened with a feeling of excitement.

Today, she thought. Today I'll be in London. She smiled as Sarah brought in the water for her to wash up.

"Good morning, Sarah," she said. "Isn't it a beautiful day?"

"Yes, Miss Caroline," she said.

"Sarah, I think I shall wear the pale blue silk with the redingote. I should like to look a little special today."

"Yes, miss," said Sarah. She took out the dress, one of Caroline's favorites. It had long puffed sleeves slashed with navy inserts and rows of navy ruching at the bottom of the skirt. The redingote was navy blue slashed with inserts of pale blue. A navy bonnet lined with pale blue silk completed the costume. She was impatient as Sarah did her hair, for she was eager to be on the way. There was a delay while Aurelia searched for a missing brooch, and it was after eleven before they began the final part of their journey.

CHAPTER 4

Caroline's first view of Woburn Square was as the sun was setting.

"Oh, how lovely it is!" she exclaimed. "Do look, Aurelia. There is a garden and trees; it does not seem as if we are in the city at all. But the houses are all of stone—and so alike—so different from the timber we are accustomed to in Lancashire. I cannot wait to explore London!"

"Yes, indeed, my love," said Aurelia. "We must engage a respectable guide who will take us on a tour of the more interesting parts of the metropolis. We need not even leave the comfort of our carriage."

Caroline smiled but did not reply. She was already stepping out of the carriage with the help of a footman. At the door she was met by a tall, rather imposing man.

"Miss Chessington?" he asked with a bow.

"Yes, I am Caroline Chessington."

"I am Briggs, butler to Mr. and Mrs. Hardy. I am pleased to be of service to you during your stay in Woburn Square."

"Thank you, Briggs." She introduced Aurelia and went inside.

Woburn Square, one of the streets in close proximity to Russell Square, the largest square in London, was an area of newly built houses, too new to be either of historical interest or fashionable. It seemed, at first glance, to be more elegant than Caroline had expected or desired. The house she had rented was a comfortable stone dwelling built in the current style made fashionable by John Nash: light and airy, with perfectly proportioned rooms. Mr. and

Mrs. Hardy had furnished it with simplicity and taste in the newly popular Regency style. Everything about it seemed new. It was so different from Brampton, where almost everything was centuries old and different styles mixed happily together in a cluttered, comfortable way. Caroline was struck by the almost modest size and style of the furniture in comparison with the massive, heavily carved pieces at Brampton. She did not, however, inspect the entire house, because she was tired from the journey. After an early dinner, she retired, promising herself to arise early the next day.

Caroline awakened the next morning eager to begin her explorations. Sarah brought her morning chocolate and pulled back the curtains.

"It's a pretty day, Miss Caroline," she said. "Did you sleep well?"

"Splendidly!" said Caroline. "Sarah, has my cousin come downstairs yet?"

Knowing what prompted the inquiry, Sarah averted her gaze and said, "No, miss. Miss Peakirk has not yet awakened. I believe she was quite tired from the journey."

"Ah," said Caroline, "then perhaps I should not dawdle in bed, but dress and be on my way. I shall wear the brown wool walking dress with the matching coat."

"Very good, Miss Caroline," was all Sarah replied, but she was pleased that her mistress intended to escape before her cousin awakened. "Always fussing and bothering Miss Caroline as if she were her mother and not a poor relation as depends on Miss Caroline's generosity," Sarah had told her sister once when she'd visited her on her half-day.

Caroline had provided herself with a guidebook and had marked several places that she most wanted to see. When she was served in the breakfast parlor, she asked Briggs about the best way to get to the British Museum and St. Paul's.

"For you know, Briggs, this is my first trip to London and I wish to see all the places of interest."

Briggs smiled in a fatherly way, for Caroline had charmed him, as she invariably did all servants.

"The British Museum is nearby, miss, but I would suggest that you take the carriage, all the same," said Briggs. "If you wish, I shall have it sent round."

"Oh, thank you, Briggs," said Caroline, "but I am accustomed to walking. I am a country girl, you know."

"But miss . . ."

"Yes, Briggs?"

"As you are new to London, I hope you won't take it amiss if I warn you to be on your guard. There are many out there who'd be happy to take advantage of your tender age."

"You needn't worry, Briggs. I'll be careful." (Oh, Lord, she thought. I've traded Cousin Aurelia for Briggs!)

After Caroline had finished her breakfast she picked up her reticule and her guidebook and set out to see London. It was a glorious spring day and there were so many places she wanted to see: the Tower, with its seven hundred years of history, starting with the Conqueror; Westminster Abbey; St. Paul's and its famous Whispering Gallery; the new gaslights in Pall Mall; the British Museum with the famed Elgin Marbles; Bond Street; St. James's were all a jumble in her mind. In true Caroline fashion, however, she was off to the British Museum first. The stories about the Elgin Marbles had piqued her curiosity and she wanted to see what had excited so much comment. After that, she would go to St. Paul's in the middle of the city.

Feeling just a bit guilty at having left Aurelia behind, but savoring her freedom, Caroline walked toward the Museum, gazing about her as she went. There were so many carriages and people about. So many houses, too, in such a small space. No one had any land. Despite the greenery of the square, Caroline thought she would miss the country if she had to stay in London permanently.

After a short walk, Caroline saw the outlines of the Museum in

Great Russell Street. She was anxious to see the Egyptian antiquities as well as the Elgin Marbles. The latter had recently been acquired by the nation from Lord Elgin, who had brought them back from the Parthenon when he was British Ambassador to Turkey.

Caroline found the room with the marbles and discovered them to be a collection of bas-reliefs, a frieze, and some statuary from the Parthenon which dealt with the goddess Minerva. She stood there looking at them, somewhat nonplussed.

"Not quite what you expected?" asked a quiet voice from behind. She turned around. The speaker, a gentleman of some thirty years, was tall and quite thin. He was dressed in a coat of super-fine navy wool which seemed a bit large, and doe-colored trousers. His shirt was of the finest linen; his collar points and cravat were neat yet fashionable. In his hands he carried a beaver hat and a gold-handled ebony cane. While he was by no means a Dandy, there was a quiet elegance about his person. Caroline liked what she saw.

"Well," she said doubtfully, "I am certain they are of great worth, and their antiquity must make them of interest to us."

"But you expected them to have all their arms?" said the man, with a smile.

"They are a bit of a disappointment," replied Caroline, returning the smile. "But indeed, London is not! There is so much to see, I am certain I could not see it all if I stayed a year!"

"You are a visitor to London, then?" asked the gentleman.

"Yes, I am here for a few months. But though I may not be from London, I do know that it is not at all the thing for me to be speaking to you when we have not been properly introduced."

The gentleman looked around the room. "There is no one here with whom I am acquainted," he said. "I shall be obliged to introduce myself. I am Giles Kendal. I am on Lord Walsingham's staff and have recently come from the Continent, where I was foolish enough to contract a most annoying illness. I am finding my convalescence a dead bore, and am reduced to visiting museums for excitement. I should very much like to present myself to you, but unfortunately, I do not know your name."

Caroline laughed. "I am Caroline Chessington," she said. "My story is not as interesting as yours. I live in Lan—in the North, and have come to London for my first visit, accompanied by the elderly cousin with whom I live."

"And whose chaperonage you have managed to escape today?"

"Oh, no," said Caroline. "I am quite accustomed to being on my own. As you can see, I am no longer a schoolgirl, Mr. Kendal."

"But hardly in your dotage," he retorted.

Realizing that the conversation, although extremely enjoyable, was most improper, Caroline strove to return to a safe topic.

"How indebted England is to Lord Elgin for having purchased these treasures," she said.

"As to that," said Mr. Kendal, obediently following her lead, "there is some debate. Lord Elgin spent fifty thousand pounds of his own fortune on the marbles, and the Government has been obliged to spend another thirty-six thousand pounds to purchase them for the Museum. Some people, vulgarians, no doubt, have questioned such an expense for inanimate objects."

"Especially ones with no arms!" said Caroline.

"Indeed, Miss Chessington, you understand the situation completely."

"I think," said Caroline, "that it is time I returned home. My cousin will be anxious about me, especially as I contrived to leave this morning before she had awakened."

"So you did escape," said Giles teasingly.

"Not at all," said Caroline. "Well, perhaps there is a little truth there. Chaperones can be quite tiresome."

"I hope, Miss Chessington, that I shall have the pleasure of making this tiresome chaperone's acquaintance. May I call on you?" As she hesitated, he added, "It would be a great kindness to me if you would permit me to show you London. You cannot imagine how dull it has been for me!"

"In that case, how can I refuse?" said Caroline. "We shall look forward to seeing you."

As they left the Museum, Giles looked around for Caroline's conveyance. "Have you no carriage?" he asked.

"Oh, no," said Caroline. "On such a lovely day, I would much prefer to walk. And it is not far."

"May I have the pleasure of seeing you home?" asked Giles.

"Thank you, Mr. Kendal," answered Caroline, looking at her fob. "Oh, dear, it is later than I thought, and I am expected home for luncheon. It is not at all necessary for you to see me home," she added.

"Not necessary, but it would give me a great deal of pleasure," answered Giles.

"In that case I will not protest, but instead will ask if you would like to join my cousin and me for lunch."

"Thank you, but I cannot. I, too, am expected home for luncheon."

"Then perhaps we should leave before our relations decide we have been spirited away."

Giles laughed. As they walked, Caroline mentioned some of the other sights she planned to see. In a short time, they were in Woburn Square. Giles again asked permission to call and made his bow.

As she took off her hat and gloves, Caroline reflected agreeably on the man she had met. He was quite charming, she thought. His manner, although sportive, did not pass the bounds of good breeding. He certainly was much more interesting than the gentlemen who had previously come her way, chosen for her by Lady Skipton or other matchmaking mamas. And he was rather attractive, although his illness had obviously left him a trifle pale and thin. It would be nice to see him again. She hoped he would call.

Giles, for his part, was also pleased with his new acquaintance.

It was not yet the Season, and London was damnably dull. He was still not permitted to ride, and while he hated his invalidish role, he was forced to admit that he tired easily. It would be pleasant to have someone with whom to pass the long days before he could rejoin Lord Walsingham. Miss Chessington was not a beauty, but neither was she an antidote. She was obviously well bred and possessed a sense of humor, which wasn't easy to find these days. Yes, Miss Chessington seemed to be a perfectly unexceptionable young woman. A mild flirtation would do him good.

When Caroline entered the dining room, she found Aurelia already in a state over her absence.

"I was most distressed, my love, to discover that you had gone out unattended. In a strange city! Only consider how improper it must appear."

"To whom, Aurelia? No one knows who I am."

"Exactly, my love. And until you have established yourself, you would not wish to give the impression that you are not well bred, or that you are fast. It is not the same in London as it is at Brampton. You must be more careful."

"Aurelia, please recollect that I do not mean to establish myself, as you put it. In any event, you will be pleased to know that I have already made an acquaintance in London. It is a gentleman and he has asked permission to call."

"A gentleman!" remonstrated Aurelia. "Surely, Caroline, you have not been speaking to a man to whom you have not been properly introduced!"

"Indeed, Aurelia," said Caroline wearily, "if I am not to speak to anyone until I am introduced, how am I to meet anyone? Mr. Kendal seemed perfectly respectable: he is attached to Lord Walsingham's staff and is on convalescent leave. He intends to call on you and introduce himself, which I am persuaded he would not do if he had evil designs on my person."

"Caroline, pray tell me that you did not speak to a strange gen-

tleman in that funning way you have. He would not understand
that you have such an odd way of expressing yourself. Did you
say that he is attached to Lord Walsingham? That seems quite
unexceptionable. I wonder if he is related to Lord Kimborough;
for you must know that their family name is Kendal."

"No, I didn't know that."

"The Kimboroughs are of the best *ton*. Lord Kimborough is an
earl, and Lady Kimborough was a Halland, daughter of the Earl
of Malton."

"Good God, Aurelia, you seem to have made a study of them!"
exclaimed Caroline.

"I have always kept abreast of the peerage," said Aurelia with
a sniff. "One never knows when such information may prove useful. You see it has, for you have already made the acquaintance
of one of the family. Of course, it must have been the younger
son if he introduced himself as Mr. Kendal. A pity, my love, for
the Kimboroughs are not very wealthy, and a younger son, without a title . . ."

"How you do go on, Aurelia," said Caroline. "We do not even
know if Mr. Kendal is of the same family. It is not an uncommon
name. As we have just met, I think it is premature to be counting
his fortune. As for a title, I have told you that I am not on the
lookout for a title. Perhaps Mr. Kendal will not even call on us.
If he knew how you were plotting, I am very certain he would
not!"

CHAPTER 5

Either Mr. Kendal remained in ignorance of Aurelia's plotting or was undeterred by it, because he presented himself in Woburn Square on the afternoon after his meeting with Caroline. The ladies were seated in the library, Aurelia reading the *Gazette* and Caroline her guidebook.

"Mr. Giles Kendal," announced Briggs. The ladies looked up as he entered. He was again quietly elegant in a brown coat with fawn trousers. His brown hair was combed in the military manner, and he looked to Aurelia exactly as a young gentleman should.

"How do you do, Mr. Kendal?" said Caroline with a smile. "It is so nice to see you again. May I present my cousin, Miss Peakirk?"

"How do you do, Miss Peakirk?" asked Giles. He kissed her hand. Caroline suppressed a grin, for this gesture, out of fashion with the young, was exactly the sort of thing calculated to appeal to Aurelia. Mr. Kendal's diplomatic training showed.

"So pleased, Mr. Kendal," said Aurelia. "Dear Caroline has told me so much about you. I collect that you are on Lord Walsingham's staff in Vienna. How exciting that must be."

"Actually, Miss Peakirk, it is rather a quiet spot at this time. Since the War ended, we aides are more likely to be called upon to chaperone the ambassador's daughter than to carry out a diplomatic mission."

"Your family must be so pleased to have you restored to them," said Aurelia.

"Aurelia," said Caroline in a warning tone.

"Indeed, ma'am, I fear that a tiresome invalid is not the most welcome of visitors, even if one is a son of the household."

"Oh, Mr. Kendal, I cannot believe that your mama was not delighted to have you home. Any mother must be proud to have a son such as you," she concluded archly.

"Mr. Kendal," interrupted Caroline, "I have been studying my guidebook most carefully. I should very much like to see the Waterloo Bridge. I understand it is near completion."

"Yes, the dedication is set for June. If you and Miss Peakirk intend to remain in London, I should be honored to have you as my guests at the ceremony. My leave extends until the end of June."

"Oh, Mr. Kendal, how very kind of you . . . so delighted . . ." began Aurelia.

"Thank you, Mr. Kendal," said Caroline. "We would like that." Her smile indicated her pleasure at the invitation.

"It will be my pleasure, Miss Chessington." He stood up. "I am afraid I have stayed too long," he said. He bowed to Aurelia as he said, "Miss Peakirk, your obedient. Miss Chessington, yours." He turned and left.

Aurelia barely waited until he was out of the room before she spoke.

"Caroline, such a gentleman," she said. "Such address, such elegance of manner. He stayed no longer than was proper. I certainly hope, my love, that you intend to encourage Mr. Kendal."

"Cousin Aurelia, if I were to see Mr. Kendal again, that would be lovely. If I were never to see him again, it would be unfortunate, but I am certain I should recover. I most certainly do not intend to seek Mr. Kendal's attention, nor can I. I am tired of having every young man who speaks to me immediately selected for my husband. If you will excuse me, I have some things to attend to."

After Caroline had left, Aurelia said with a start, "Gracious! I never did find out if he is related to the Kimboroughs!"

When Giles entered his family's house on Grosvenor Street, he found his mother seated in the parlor, reading a letter.

"Did you have a pleasant afternoon, my love?" she asked. "I hope you have not tired yourself."

"And risk a scolding from you?" he replied teasingly, kissing her on the cheek.

"I wish you did not still look so pale and tired," said his mother. "I cannot like you racketing about, but then you always were the most stubborn of my children." She patted the place next to her invitingly. "Come, dearest, and do sit down. It seems we are to have a visitor, which should make your days a little less dull."

"A visitor?" asked Giles. "Not Cecilia and those noisy brats of hers?"

Ignoring these very improper comments about his sister and her children, his mother said, "Yes, I have had a letter from Lavinia Chedworth. Such an age since I have seen her! You must know that she is bringing out Arabella this Season. She had intended to bring Arabella to town this month to have fittings for her gowns, but one of the younger children has contracted measles and Lavinia feels she cannot leave at this time. As Arabella is my goddaughter, Lavinia has asked me if Arabella might stay with us until she can come to London. Naturally, I shall write to her and tell her we would be delighted to have Arabella with us."

"Arabella," said Giles. "Wasn't she the one with spots?"

"Well, I must admit that she was not very promising as a child, but Lavinia says she has blossomed into quite a beauty."

"Depend on it," said Giles cynically, "if her mother says she's a beauty, she probably still has spots."

"Dearest, how unkind of you! In any event, I shall rely on you to help put Arabella at her ease. So nice to have a son in the Diplomatic!"

"I do believe you're trying to flatter me, Mama," said Giles. "You have my word that I shall be kind to your guest, even if she has spots and squints."

"No, dearest, I believe it was the next daughter, Maria, who squinted. But I daresay she will improve as well."

Giles, stifling a grin, kissed his mother again and announced that he was going to his room to rest before dinner.

"An excellent idea, Giles," said his mother, already preoccupied with plans for Miss Chedworth's entertainment.

Giles, escaping to his bedroom, allowed himself a chuckle at his mother's conversation. He dismissed his man and stretched out on the bed. His thoughts were not of the approaching visit of his mother's goddaughter, but of his afternoon visit to Woburn Square. He suspected that the elderly cousin had been trying to discover who he was; she might even have an idea that his father was the Earl of Kimborough. Miss Chessington, however, had shown no interest in his family; in fact, she had changed the subject when her cousin had probed too closely. Giles wondered about Caroline Chessington. He was unaccustomed to such a lack of interest in his pedigree. She did not at all seem to be on the catch for a husband, which was unusual enough to be refreshing. Her lively wit was a welcome change from the tiresome cosseting which was the invalid's lot, and her lack of flirtatiousness made her comfortable to be with.

He wondered, too, about her background. She lived in a quiet area where the *ton* would not be found, but Woburn Square was an acceptable address. Her dress was simple, but Giles knew from experience that there was nothing to be faulted in either the cut or the fabric of her gown. She had an air of breeding and of one accustomed to being attended to. She was unacquainted with London, which meant that she had not been there for her comeout, and Giles could not recall mention of the Chessington name in Society. He was still trying to puzzle out Miss Chessington's history when he fell asleep.

CHAPTER 6

Arabella arrived in Grosvenor Street two weeks after her mother's letter had reached Lady Kimborough. She was accompanied by her maid and two outriders, as her mama was fearful of permitting a delicately nurtured young female to make such a lengthy journey unattended. When Giles arrived home that afternoon, he found the front hall full of bandboxes and baggage. He went into the parlor and found his mother entertaining a veritable beauty. Arabella had certainly outgrown her spots and had developed into a young woman of uncommon good looks. Her blond curls, peeking out from under a fetching blue poke bonnet, perfectly framed her heart-shaped face. She was dressed in a charmingly simple white-and-blue dress, topped by a blue pelisse. She turned as Giles entered the room and he had a vision of large, sparkling blue eyes and a dimple on a complexion of pink and white.

"Giles, my love," said his mother in a mildly reproving voice. Giles realized that he must be staring. "You do remember my dear goddaughter, Arabella Chedworth? I daresay you have not seen her since she was in the schoolroom."

"No, indeed, ma'am, I have not, and it is my misfortune," replied Giles, smiling at Arabella. She blushed prettily.

"It is so kind of your dear mama to have me," she said. "Poor Mama was so distracted. Not only did Maria contract measles, but John and Lydia too. Papa was most displeased. Fortunately, I had had them when I was a child. I did not want to leave Mama, but she insisted. I am very happy to be here."

"And we are delighted to have you, my dear," said Lady Kimborough. "I think perhaps I shall have you shown to your room. After your fatiguing journey, I am certain you would like to rest before dinner."

"Yes, please," said Arabella. "I am quite tired."

Lady Kimborough rang the servants' bell and Hayle, the butler, appeared.

"My lady?" he said.

"Hayle, please have Miss Chedworth shown to her chamber," said Lady Kimborough.

"Yes, my lady," he replied. "This way, miss," he said to Arabella.

Arabella kissed her godmother and smiled at Giles.

"Have a pleasant rest, my dear," said Lady Kimborough.

"Oh, I know I shall," said Arabella.

"Perhaps tomorrow I can take you for a ride in the carriage to show you London," said Giles.

"Oh, that would be lovely," said Arabella, blushing again. She followed Hayle out of the room.

"What a delightful child!" said Lady Kimborough when Arabella had gone.

"She is a beauty," replied Giles. "I predict she will become all the rage. I have not seen a lovelier face in many a Season."

Lady Kimborough peered sharply at her son. She had long felt it time for him to marry; as a younger son without an independent fortune, he would have to marry money. Arabella's fortune was comfortable; while she was not an heiress, she would be considered more than eligible. Lady Kimborough had never before considered her son and her goddaughter, because Arabella had been a child and Giles's taste had never run to young girls just out of the schoolroom. But if he should be taken by her. . . . No doubt Lavinia Chedworth had designs on a title for her lovely daughter, but Lavinia was good-natured. If her daughter wished to marry the younger son of an earl, she would not forbid it. . . . Lady Kimborough ended her musings.

"How nice of you to offer to escort Arabella in your carriage, dear," she said. "However, you must remember that she is not yet out, and it would not do to have her appear coming or fast. I think, however, that if you would offer to escort her when she goes shopping with her maid, that would be unexceptionable."

"Go shopping!" exclaimed Giles. "You cannot be serious. Surely, as she is your goddaughter, I can take her in the carriage for a ride in the Park without exciting comment."

"Nevertheless, Giles," said Lady Kimborough, "great care must be taken. We have a responsibility to the Chedworths, and I will not have tongues wagging while Arabella is under my protection."

"Have no fear, Mama," answered Giles, kissing his mother's cheek. "I shall be on my best behavior."

CHAPTER 7

Caroline had not abandoned her plans for improving the agricultural methods at Brampton, and she decided to visit Stokes to discuss some of the business arrangements. Ordinarily she would have requested that Stokes call on her in Woburn Square, but she did not care to have Aurelia question her about her plans. She waited until Aurelia had retired to her room for her nap one afternoon and then, dressed in a sober gray walking dress and spencer, set out for Stokes's office in the City.

When Caroline entered the office the clerk stared in surprise. Well-bred females, in his experience, did not visit a man of business. She told him, in her cool voice, that Miss Chessington wished to see Mr. Stokes. He mumbled an inarticulate "Yes, ma'am," and disappeared behind a door. He very well knew that Miss Chessington was one of his employer's favored clients. In a few moments, the door opened and Mr. Stokes came out.

"My dear Miss Chessington," he exclaimed. "I would have been most happy to call on you. It was certainly not necessary for you to trouble yourself by coming to my office."

"Indeed, it was no trouble, Mr. Stokes," replied Caroline.

"Please come into my private office," said Mr. Stokes. He ushered her into the room. As he closed the door he said to the clerk, "I do not wish to be disturbed."

"I did not like to say this in front of the staff, Miss Chessington," he continued as he sat down behind his desk, "and I hope you will not take it amiss, but you are unfamiliar with London ways. It would be better in the future if you requested me to call on you."

"I am not a schoolgirl, Mr. Stokes. I am accustomed to being in charge of my own affairs. However," she said with a smile, "if it makes you feel better I will tell you that I had a special reason for calling on you in your office. But first I must thank you for your excellent choice of the house in Woburn Square. It is most comfortable and the servants are taking very good care of us."

"It is good of you to say so, Miss Chessington," said Mr. Stokes. "I am pleased that it is to your liking. Are you enjoying your stay in London?"

"Oh, yes, Mr. Stokes," said Caroline. "I am finding there is so much to see. I have been to the British Museum and St. Paul's and even the Palace. London is a fascinating city. But it is not of London that I wish to speak."

"How may I serve you, Miss Chessington?"

"As you know, I have long been concerned with improving Brampton. I have read Tull's *Horse Hoeing Husbandry,* Horn's *Gentleman Farmer,* and Weston's *New System of Agriculture,* and I wish to introduce some of their methods. I should like to discuss with you financial arrangements for draining and enclosing several acres."

"But my dear Miss Chessington!" exclaimed Stokes, slightly stunned. "Surely your steward is the proper person to attend to such matters! There is no need to trouble yourself."

"My steward is an excellent man, but somewhat old-fashioned. He has a melancholy way of staring at his hands and clucking his disapproval at my newfangled notions whenever I approach him about improvements. As he has been at Brampton since before I was born and is most sincerely attached to my interests, I could never consider pensioning him off. Therefore, I have decided to broach the matter myself."

"But you cannot have made a study of these matters! I am not an agricultural man myself, but I know they are quite complicated."

"As I said, I have been reading quite a bit," said Caroline, "although there is much that I do not understand. I have written to Mr. Coke of Norfolk and to Mr. Young, who are most intrigued to find a female with an interest in agriculture. They have supplied me with a great deal of very useful information and I begin to see how much there is to be done at Brampton."

"You are a most unusual female, Miss Chessington, if I may say so."

"Well, you know, Mr. Stokes, I have been virtually on my own for a long while now. What a dull life I would lead if I sat home all day doing needlework!"

"Exactly how much money do you think will be required, Miss Chessington?" asked Mr. Stokes somewhat apprehensively.

"I have made a list of the items which I think would be helpful at Brampton." She reached into her reticule and pulled out a piece of paper. "Here it is," she said as she handed it to him. "You will see that I have estimated approximately how much each item will cost. The total sum is at the bottom."

Mr. Stokes put on his glasses. "Hmm," he said, as he scanned the list. "That's quite a sum. Quite a sum indeed."

"But I do have it?" questioned Caroline.

"Oh, indeed," said Mr. Stokes. "You have it and to spare. But I cannot advise you to spend such a sum on newfangled techniques which next year someone will decide are not nearly as good as those which are tried and true!"

"As you say, Mr. Stokes, you are not an agricultural man. I am certain that if you were to come to Brampton, you would see the need for these measures. I do not believe things have changed since my grandfather's time! Please consider the best way to arrange matters so as to be most advantageous to the estate." She stood up and held out her hand.

"Come, Mr. Stokes, we are old friends, after all. You have advised me wisely and well. You know I would not foolishly jeopardize my fortune. I am certain I can count on you to prevent that." She smiled.

Mr. Stokes thawed. "I am not saying that I approve of this plan, Miss Chessington," he said, "but you have always commanded my respect."

"Thank you, Mr. Stokes," said Caroline graciously. "I shall expect to hear from you."

"Yes, of course," said Mr. Stokes. "It may take some time, however, to work out the details. I will call on you then."

"That will be fine," said Caroline as she preceded Stokes into the anteroom. "I shall look forward to hearing from you." As she turned to leave, she noticed a man seated.

"Mr. Bradford!" exclaimed Mr. Stokes. "I was not expecting you today." There was a slight note of dismay in his voice.

"But it seems, Mr. Stokes, that I chose the perfect day on which to make my visit." He smiled at Caroline as he came forward. "It is indeed a rare thing to see such loveliness in this part of town. Surely you will introduce me."

Mr. Stokes could scarcely refuse the introduction, although it was clearly not to his liking.

"Miss Chessington," he said reluctantly, "may I present Adrian Bradford? Mr. Bradford is also a client."

Caroline held out her hand. "How do you do?" she asked. "It is very nice to meet you."

"The pleasure, Miss Chessington, is all mine."

"And now I am afraid I must be going," said Caroline.

"May I have the honor of seeing you to your carriage, Miss Chessington?"

Mr. Stokes coughed slightly.

"I believe Mr. Stokes is waiting to see you," said Caroline. "I do not wish to keep you." She smiled at the two men and swept out the door.

"What a delightful female!" said Adrian Bradford.

"Please come into my office, Mr. Bradford," said Stokes, disapproval registering in his voice.

When they were seated, Mr. Bradford said to Stokes, "Come, tell me about that intriguing female. Who is she? If she came alone, she must be wealthy. We're old friends; you can tell me."

"You should know, Mr. Bradford, that I would never discuss one client with another. It would violate my professional responsibilities."

"Still the pompous stuffed shirt I remember from my childhood," said Mr. Bradford. "Come, come, Stokes," he wheedled. "You know I need to marry an heiress. Perhaps your Miss Chessington is just what I've been looking for."

"Mr. Bradford, my sincere attachment to your honored parents and my family's long association with yours, prevent me from stating my feelings. However, I must tell you that the course which you are pursuing is disastrous. If you do not cease the spending of money which you do not have, you shall be ruined. It is as simple as that."

"That," said Adrian Bradford patiently, "is why I have to marry an heiress. If you are so attached to my interests, you should be helping me to meet one instead of prosing on about things over which I have no control."

Mr. Stokes's eyes started out of their sockets.

"Mr. Bradford!" he exclaimed. "I cannot believe what I am hearing. If your late parents could hear you . . ." He wrung his hands.

"If my father had not left those provisions in his will denying me access to my fortune for another five years, I would not be facing ruin now!" interrupted Adrian. He stood up. "If I had known you were going to give me a lecture, I wouldn't have come." He turned and strode out of the room. The door slammed shut behind him.

"Indeed!" exclaimed Mr. Stokes. "Indeed! That the Bradfords

—such an old and distinguished family—should come to this."
He shook his head. "I never thought I would see this day."

By the time he had reached the street, Adrian's anger had dissipated. His temper was erratic, but he found anger difficult to sustain and he never held a grudge. He tried to think of how he could turn the meeting with Miss Chessington to good account. The first thing was to find out more about her. Single young women of his acquaintance did not frequent the business offices of the City. Only one in charge of her own affairs would make such a visit. Only one secure in her position would risk the disapprobation of Society. What but a great fortune could give her this security? Neither a great name nor great beauty explained it. No, he must find out more about her, and the place to start was Stokes's office.

As Adrian thought, he slowly mounted the stairs to Stokes's office again. He opened the door slightly and looked inside. Stokes's door was closed and he appeared to be talking with that fuss-budget assistant of his. Only the clerk was in the outer office. Before going inside, Adrian removed his gloves and put them inside his jacket. He then went inside. The clerk looked up as he entered.

"Crippen, I seem to have misplaced my gloves. Have you seen them?"

"No, sir, I can't say as I have," replied the clerk.

"How very annoying," said Adrian. "I can scarcely go to Lady Effington's without my gloves."

"No, sir," said the clerk.

"By the by," said Adrian, approaching the clerk, "a fine-looking woman, Miss Chessington. I would really like to know more about her."

"I can't tell you anything about her, sir," said Crippen. "It would be worth my job." He looked expectant.

Adrian held out a sovereign and slipped it into the clerk's palm. "Can you tell me about her now?"

Crippen looked at the gold coin in his hand and carefully shifted it to his pocket. "Miss Chessington," he said woodenly, "is an heiress. From Lancashire, she is. Worth a ransom, but she don't want anyone to know that she's so plump in the pocket."

"Whyever not?" exclaimed Adrian. "If I had a fortune, I'd certainly let everyone know!"

Crippen held out his hand. Adrian looked at it and slipped another coin into it.

"I overheard Old Stokesy telling Potts that she wants to be liked for herself and not for her money," continued Crippen as he transferred the new coin to his pocket. "Myself, I can't say I see it."

Adrian was much in sympathy with this sentiment. "Know where she lives, Crippen?" he asked.

Crippen was silent as he looked at Adrian. Adrian, exasperated, pulled out a third coin and handed it to Crippen.

"No, sir, I'm afraid I don't," he said as he slipped the coin into his bulging pocket.

Adrian looked at him in amazement. "Why, you thief!" he exclaimed. He stormed out of the office, slamming the door a second time. The noise brought Mr. Stokes and his assistant to the door.

"What's going on here, Crippen?" asked Stokes sternly.

"Nuthin', sir."

"Who was at the door then?"

"Just Mr. Bradford looking for his gloves, sir. He's right excitable. When I didn't have them, he slammed the door."

"All right then, Crippen, back to work. There's much to be done."

"Yes, sir," replied Crippen. As Stokes and Potts went back into the office, Crippen patted his pocket complacently.

Adrian's anger lasted a little longer this time, but he had to smile wryly at the way he'd been outmaneuvered. His mind shifted quickly to the more pressing problem of meeting Miss Chessington. Damn it, he didn't even know her first name. If she were an heiress—and if that dratted clerk were telling the truth! —she should be seen riding in the Park or at some of the *ton* parties. It was still before the Season, but some early-comers to town had already begun the rounds of parties and routs. He'd have to start going again to those boring affairs, toadeating dowagers and flattering matrons. And that required a wardrobe, for it was fatal to look as if one were worried about money. His tailor was becoming more insistent about being paid. If he didn't meet an heiress soon and bring her to the altar, he'd have to leave the country. He was desperate.

CHAPTER 8

Caroline did not spend all of her time in London visiting historical sights or discussing business. Giles Kendal had called several times in Woburn Square and Caroline increasingly looked forward to his visits. He had a wry sense of humor and his descriptions of Society in Vienna were amusing. He often brought a book he thought she would enjoy or marked a passage in the paper which he thought would be of interest. He seemed to appreciate her comments as well, as though she had something of worth to contribute. Caroline, accustomed to the insincere compliments of fortune hunters, was pleased to be treated as an intelligent, thinking woman.

She had discovered, too, the many pleasures London had to offer and was surprised to find herself enjoying them so much. While she had no entrée to Almack's and had no desire to be seen at that bastion of matchmaking mamas, Giles had squired her to some of the other diversions available. They had viewed a balloon ascension, and Giles had taken them to the theater, the ballet, and the opera. They had seen Kean as Hamlet and Madame Pasta in *Le Nozze di Figaro* at the King's Theatre, which was, according to her guidebook, one of London's most fashionable centers of entertainment. She found Giles Kendal stimulating and looked forward to his visits; she was, therefore, dismayed when those visits suddenly became less frequent. She had finally begun to feel that special sense of companionship, of pleasure in someone's company, that she had been certain would always elude her. She had no explanation for his seeming loss of interest, but was too proud to ask him for one. She merely shrugged her shoulders and continued as she always had, making her own enjoyment and living her own life.

Two weeks after her visit to Mr. Stokes, Caroline and Aurelia were scheduled to attend a performance of the opera. As Caroline descended the stairs, Aurelia regarded her approvingly.

"My love, you look charmingly," she said, eyeing Caroline's dress of cerise-striped silk gauze. "And that hairdo! I was not at all certain about it when you described it, but it looks most becoming." The Psyche knot interlaced with cerise ribbons indeed set off Caroline's face becomingly.

"Thank you, ma'am," said Caroline. "And may I say that you are also in high looks tonight?"

"Well, I do think this gown flatters me," said Aurelia, smoothing it down. "Mauve was always a good color for me. All ladies, you know, cannot wear mauve. And do you like the turban? It matches so perfectly, don't you think?"

"Oh, yes, the match is indeed excellent," said Caroline, admirably maintaining her composure. "Shall we go, Aurelia? We do not want to be late."

"No," said Aurelia, "although one would not want to be too early. It would be so unfashionable and would stamp us as mere provincial nobodies."

"We are provincial nobodies," said Caroline with a laugh. "But have no fear. If we leave now—and the carriage is waiting—we shall just be seated in time for the curtain." She started for the door. Aurelia, her fan in one hand and her reticule in the other, followed.

As Caroline had predicted, they reached their seats only a few minutes before the opera began. Aurelia did not seem to concentrate on the performance, being more interested in discovering who was there and what the other women were wearing.

"Look, Caroline, there is Lady Sheppingham," she whispered. "Oh, I wish the lights were on so I could see if she's wearing the Sheppingham rubies."

"Oh, hush, Aurelia," replied Caroline in an undertone. "I'm certain you're disturbing the other people."

"Indeed you are, madam," said an annoyed voice from behind. Caroline stifled a laugh, but Aurelia began fanning herself in embarrassment. However, she remained silent for the remainder of the first act.

When the lights went on for the intermission, Caroline and Aurelia strolled out into the foyer. Here Aurelia could gaze to her heart's content. Even Caroline was amazed at the gown on one of the women, not realizing that a box at the King's Theatre was the "shop window" of the Cyprians and that it was Harriette Wilson herself who was the object of her scrutiny.

"I must say I think that gown is quite revealing," Caroline was saying when a man came up behind her.

"Dare I believe my eyes?" he asked. "Can it be Miss Chessington?"

Caroline turned around. Standing there was Adrian Bradford.

"Yes, I am Caroline Chessington. And you, I believe, are the gentleman I met in Mr. Stokes's office."

"Adrian Bradford," he said. "I did not expect you to remember my name and I am honored that you remembered my face."

Aurelia made a small noise in her throat and Caroline remembered her presence.

"Aurelia, may I present Mr. Bradford? Mr. Bradford, my cousin, Miss Peakirk."

Aurelia held out her hand. "Delighted, Mr. Bradford," she said. "Did you not say you met Caroline in the office of her man of business?"

"It was some weeks ago, Aurelia," interrupted Caroline. "I had to speak to him about something at home."

"But I cannot imagine his not coming to see you," said Aurelia. "Surely you did not have to see him in his office?"

"Ah, but it was seeing Miss Chessington in such an unlikely setting which intrigued me, Miss Peakirk. It is so rare to see a female with a head for business matters."

"Oh, how right you are, Mr. Bradford," tittered Aurelia. "I myself have no understanding at all of business. My dear father used to tell me I was his silly widgeon. But Caroline—so extraordinary, really—has always been interested in business. She takes such an interest in the running of Br—"

"I think the performance is about to begin again," interrupted Caroline, trying to stop Aurelia from giving away the name of her home.

"May I see you home?" asked Adrian. "I remember that the last time you refused me. I hope you will not refuse me again. I shall be so hurt!"

Caroline smiled. "I believe there is an actor in your past," she said. "However, we must decline as we have already made arrangements."

"Then may I call on you tomorrow?" he asked. "Surely you cannot refuse a proper request? Miss Peakirk, I appeal to you to use your influence with Miss Chessington."

"Oh," said Aurelia, "we would be honored to have you call on us, wouldn't we, Caroline?"

Caroline laughed. "We would be happy to see you tomorrow, Mr. Bradford." She gave him her address.

"Until tomorrow then," said Adrian. He bowed. "I shall see you both then." He took Aurelia's hand and kissed it.

"Such a charming man!" exclaimed Aurelia as they returned to their seats. "So handsome as well! And dressed with such elegance and refinement. Bradford, you say? The Bradford family is quite unexceptionable. I wonder if he is of that family. Why did you not tell me you had made his acquaintance?"

"I did not think of it," said Caroline. "I believe you had the same feelings about Mr. Kendal, but we have not seen him in several weeks. Come, the curtain is about to rise."

Adrian returned to his seat elated. He had spent the last two weeks looking for Caroline Chessington, to no avail. He had gone riding in the early morning on a horse that could think of nothing but its breakfast, he had promenaded in his aunt's carriage at the fashionable hour while his aunt scolded him, and he had called on dowagers of his acquaintance to learn what he could of Miss Chessington. He had discovered nothing. No one had heard of a newcomer to London named Chessington. If she were an heiress, she had certainly managed to keep it well concealed. Certainly that companion of hers would not add to her consequence. He knew how to get around that type; he'd certainly danced attendance on enough elderly females. Adrian knew the neighborhood in which they lived to be respectable but not fashionable; he hoped that Stokes's clerk had not been playing off one of his tricks. If she were wealthy, none of that mattered—not even if her fortune had been built on trade. How fortunate that he'd come to the opera tonight, after he'd almost given up hope of finding her! Caroline, her name was. It suited her. Well, he'd found her. Now he had to see if he could win her.

While they were returning home, Caroline looked at Aurelia and said, "I wonder if I should have encouraged Mr. Bradford. We know nothing of him."

"As I said, my love, the Bradfords are such an old family."

"But we do not even know if Mr. Bradford is of the same family. And even if he is, he may be totally unsuitable."

"I shouldn't think so, my love. He seemed so respectable. His manners were quite pleasing."

"I thought he seemed a bit fawning, did you not?"

"Not at all, my love. I believe you mistook his address, his gentlemanliness, for something else. He seemed quite taken with you."

"Actually, I think he seemed more taken with you," Caroline said teasingly.

"Oh, no, my love, although he did seem to find my conversation amusing. He laughed a number of times."

"Yes, ma'am, I am certain the laughter was directed entirely at you."

Aurelia blushed. "If you are not careful, my love," she said playfully, "I shall cut you out!" She giggled. Caroline, with great restraint, did not succumb to a fit of laughter until she was safely behind her own closed door.

CHAPTER 9

The next day, when Adrian arrived, he was shown in to the library, where the ladies were seated. They took note again of his blond good looks, shown to advantage by his well-cut coat and tight-fitting pantaloons. His hair, cut in the Brutus style, shone like burnished gold. While they partook of some refreshments they spoke of the Opera, the anticipated arrival of a Royal heir, and the scandalous behavior of the Royal Dukes: Clarence, in the market for a wife if the Government would provide for his ten illegitimate children, and Kent, in the twenty-seventh year of an arrangement with Mme. St. Laurent. Adrian judged this to be just the sort of conversation likely to appeal to Aurelia. He had just begun to steer the conversation to more personal concerns when Giles Kendal was announced. A momentary look of dismay crossed Adrian's face, but it was quickly erased. Giles, for his part, was surprised to find Aurelia and Caroline with a gentleman with whom he was acquainted, though slightly. He recognized the man as Adrian Bradford; their fathers had been friends at Eton, but the two sons had never been on more than nodding terms.

"Mr. Kendal," exclaimed Aurelia. "How nice to see you. Why, Caroline was saying only last night . . ."

"Mr. Kendal, are you acquainted with Mr. Bradford?" asked Caroline, not wishing Aurelia to complete the thought. She turned to Adrian. "Mr. Kendal was the first person I met in London and he made me feel quite welcome."

"Indeed," replied Adrian. "Mr. Kendal and I are old friends."

"How nice," exclaimed Aurelia. "Mr. Kendal, will you have some refreshments?"

"Thank you, no. I have recently eaten. My mother is entertaining a houseguest—a girl just out of the schoolroom who is about to make her come-out. It seems that we are forever eating some meal or other! I shall return to Lord Walsingham's as fat as a flawn."

Everyone smiled.

"So that is why we have not seen you recently, Mr. Kendal," said Aurelia.

"I have been quite busy with Miss Chedworth," said Giles. "I predict she will become all the rage this Season. Her beauty is something quite out of the ordinary."

"Beauty is, of course, a prerequisite to success in the marriage mart," said Adrian, "but I have often noticed that a fortune can overcome a tendency to freckle or a deplorable figure."

"How cynical you are, Mr. Bradford," commented Caroline.

"It is a cynicism born of experience, Miss Chessington," he replied.

"Have your experiences with heiresses been so dreadful, Mr. Bradford?" asked Aurelia archly.

"It is unfortunate, Miss Peakirk, that so often heiresses' hearts are not as big as their fortunes. Having learned my lesson, I now look for those qualities in a woman likely to prove more lasting than her fortune."

"It is refreshing to meet a man not consumed with the desire to marry an heiress," commented Caroline. "I mean—I understand that many heiresses are forever the target of fortune hunters."

"Heiresses, Miss Chessington, are not the only targets," said Giles dryly. "Matchmaking mamas have been known to consider a man's wealth or title in choosing a husband for their daughters."

"That is true," conceded Caroline, "and I consider it just as deplorable."

Adrian stood up. "I must be going," he said. "I hope to see you again soon." He kissed Aurelia's hand and bowed. "Miss Peakirk, your obedient. Miss Chessington, yours. Kendal." He turned and left.

When he was gone, Giles looked at Caroline.

"If I may ask, Miss Chessington, where did you meet Adrian Bradford?"

"I was introduced to him, Mr. Kendal. Why do you ask?"

"I hope you will understand, Miss Chessington, that only my concern for one unfamiliar with London and Society would permit me to interfere in matters properly not my affair. I must tell you that Mr. Bradford has a reputation of being a spendthrift and he is known to have gone through a considerable fortune of his own. He is said to be on the look-out for a wealthy wife."

"Then I cannot think why he would be interested in me, Mr. Kendal," said Caroline.

"You misunderstand me; I do not mean to intimate that Bradford's interest in you is for that reason. However, I believe you should be aware of his reputation. I would not speak of it if the facts were not widely known."

"I do thank you for your concern," said Caroline coolly. "However, I think that I can judge for myself Mr. Bradford's intentions." She did not add, that this was the first time that Adrian Bradford had called, nor that since his own calls had become so infrequent of late, she resented his interference in her affairs.

"Shall I order some more refreshments?" interjected Aurelia.

"Thank you, but I must take my leave," said Giles, standing. "I have not forgotten my promise to take you to the opening of the Waterloo Bridge."

"We are so looking forward to it, Mr. Kendal," said Aurelia.

"Yes, we are," said Caroline with a smile, feeling that perhaps she had been ungracious.

Giles returned the smile. "I am afraid I shall be quite busy in the next few weeks, but I hope I am able to see you again before the opening."

"That would be lovely," replied Caroline.

After Giles had gone, Caroline thought about his warning. It was quite out of character for a man of his reserve and breeding to speak as he had; it must have cost him a great deal. He was obviously trying to warn her away from Adrian Bradford, for what purposes she was not certain. She wondered if it could be jealousy and laughed at herself for her conceit. Still, she thought, it was an odd circumstance and it continued to puzzle her.

Caroline had expressed to Adrian an interest in seeing the Tower of London, so she was not surprised when he called several days later to invite her to accompany him there that afternoon. When Adrian arrived, Briggs showed him in to the parlor to await Caroline. He found Aurelia already there.

"Mr. Bradford, how nice to see you again," she said.

"You are looking as lovely as ever, Miss Peakirk," said Adrian. "I think perhaps you will be the rage of the Season."

"Oh, Mr. Bradford," tittered Aurelia. "You quite put me on the blush."

"Blushing seems a lost art these days," replied Adrian. "How delightful to see such a skillful practitioner."

Before Aurelia could respond, Caroline came into the room.

"How do you do, Mr. Bradford?" she said.

"I am fine, and I needn't ask how you are, Miss Chessington."

"Ah, Mr. Bradford is so truly the gentleman, Caroline," said Aurelia.

"Yes, he is," said Caroline.

"I think we had better be going, Miss Chessington, for there is much to see and the Tower will close."

"Yes, certainly," said Caroline. "I am sorry you are too tired to accompany us, Aurelia. Have a pleasant afternoon."

"And you, too, my love," said Aurelia archly. "Good day, Mr. Bradford."

"Good day, Miss Peakirk," said Adrian as he made an elegant bow. Then he and Caroline went to the carriage that Adrian had hired on his extended credit.

"You have certainly made a conquest in my cousin, Mr. Bradford," said Caroline.

"You must forgive me, Miss Chessington, if I seem to be fawning. However, I have met elderly female relations before, and I know the sort of flattery you would disdain is most acceptable to them. I speak in fulsome terms to Miss Peakirk to win her as an ally."

"I beg you not to speak so, Mr. Bradford. Our acquaintance is of too short a standing. Let us please just enjoy this afternoon. I read in my book that the last person to be executed here was Lord Lovat. That was in 1747—less than seventy years ago. Fancy that!"

Taking his cue from Caroline, Adrian channeled the conversation away from personal matters. When he had discovered that Caroline wished to see the Tower, he had made a visit there, acquainting himself with some of its points of interest. He took her to the Lion Tower, where the royal menagerie was kept, and Caroline was delighted with her first glimpse of an elephant. Caroline shivered at the Scaffold Site, where three queens—Anne Boleyn, Catherine Howard, and Jane Grey—had died.

"How horrible," she said with a shudder, "to die in such a way."

"It is painless because death is so swift," said Adrian.

"Oh, but to know as you put down your head what is about to occur—it must be a dreadful thing. I do not see how a civilized people could permit such a thing."

"Sometimes humans do not seem far removed from the primitive," said Adrian.

"That is very true," said Caroline somberly.

"But come," said Adrian, "let us not become melancholy! Did you know that a man once tried unsuccessfully to steal the Crown jewels? His attempt was considered so daring that Charles II pardoned him, granted him a pension, and restored his estates!"

"How strange!" commented Caroline.

The afternoon passed quickly and pleasurably, Caroline enjoying Adrian's witty comments on what they were seeing.

"It is so nice to have a personal guide," she said. "My guidebook is excellent in its way, but you make the Tower come alive for me."

"That is a compliment worth having," said Adrian. They smiled at each other.

When they reached Woburn Square, Adrian refused to come inside, protesting that the hour was late and she would be wishing to rest before dinner.

"You underestimate me," said Caroline.

"Then let us say that I do not wish a too-quickly-gained familiarity to breed contempt," said Adrian.

Caroline felt her heart beating with unaccustomed rapidity. She was not used to the accomplished flirting of a man far more experienced than she in the art of dalliance. She was relieved when Adrian left her at the door without making a definite appointment to see her again. She hoped to avoid seeing Aurelia before she could collect her thoughts, but Aurelia was awaiting her return in the parlor.

"Did you have an enjoyable time, my love?" she asked.

"Yes, it was most enjoyable," said Caroline.

"Is not Mr. Bradford a most charming gentleman?" she asked.

"Yes, he is," replied Caroline noncommittally. "If you'll excuse me, Aurelia, I should like to rest before dinner." It was a lie, but it was an effective excuse and she was able to make her escape.

Adrian was well pleased with the afternoon's work. He had flattered the elderly duenna and then shown Caroline a more subdued, more subtle charm. The contrast had frequently proved successful. Caroline was well on her way to thinking him a charming, witty man, and her companion would present no problem. He had not made another assignation, desiring to pique her curiosity. He intended, in fact, to stay away for about a week: enough time to make her wish to see him, but not so long as to allow her to forget him.

CHAPTER 10

Arabella had been thoroughly enjoying her visit to London. Lady Kimborough had been so kind, and it was such fun visiting dressmakers and trying on hats! Her gown for her come-out was almost ready, and Arabella thought there had never been such an exquisite dress. It was pale yellow, usually an unfortunate color for a blonde, but Arabella had found a gown exactly the color of her hair and the total effect was one of a spring flower. She was having a final fitting one afternoon when Giles came into the room.

"Behold the daffodil!" he exclaimed as he entered.

"Ah, dear Giles," said Lady Kimborough, "we would very much like a gentleman's opinion. Is not Arabella's gown most becoming? I am certain her mama will be pleased."

"I am certain all of London will be pleased," said Giles. "I have something which I hope will perfectly complete the costume." He pulled a package from inside his coat.

"For me?" asked Arabella. "Oh, Mr. Kendall!"

"Please open it," said Giles. "And as we are so nearly related, can't I prevail upon you to call me Giles?"

"Oh, yes, of course, Mr. Ken—Giles," said Arabella, opening the package. It contained an ivory fan painted in shades of white and yellow in the manner of Angelica Kauffmann.

"Oh, Giles!" exclaimed Arabella, turning her face up to meet his. "Dear Lady Kimborough, isn't this the most lovely thing? How can I thank you?"

"It is lovely, my dear," said Lady Kimborough. "Giles always has such excellent taste."

The seamstress, who had been waiting patiently while Arabella pirouetted about, displaying the fan, gave a discreet cough.

"Miss, if I'm to have this gown ready, you'll have to stand still."

"Oh, I'm so sorry," said Arabella. "How naughty of me! But I'm so excited. Everyone is so nice to me. I am certain no girl ever had a more wonderful come-out!" She stood obediently as the seamstress pinned the hem.

"Giles, my love, while Arabella is completing her fitting, I have something I wish to say to you. Will you accompany me to my sitting room?"

"Yes, of course, Mother," said Giles. He looked at Arabella again. "Will you excuse me?"

"Oh, yes," said Arabella.

"Perhaps you would like to go for a ride in the Park when you are finished here?" asked Giles.

"I'd like that very much," said Arabella, smiling shyly at him.

"Giles," said his mother, "I am waiting for you." She swept out of the room.

"I shall see you later," said Giles as he followed her.

Arabella blushed.

When Giles entered his mother's sitting room, she requested that he close the door.

"Now, Mother," he said when he had complied, "what have I done to displease you?"

"A fan, Giles?" asked his mother. "Do you not feel that perhaps that is too personal a gift? Please remember that my position as Lavinia Chedworth's stand-in is a delicate one. Arabella is in my care. I am certain her mama would not care to have her head turned before she has had a chance to meet an eligible *parti*."

"How cold-blooded it all sounds," said Giles.

"Don't be a fool, Giles," replied his mother. "You know very well that a girl just out of the schoolroom is very susceptible to an older man with a great deal of charm."

Giles chuckled, but his mother continued, "It is no secret, Giles, that your manner is engaging. Lord Walsingham would never have selected you as his aide were it not. But that is beside the point. I will not have Lavinia say that I contrived to have you engage Arabella's affections because you are a younger son who needs to marry a wealthy female!"

"Surely you are exaggerating, Mama," said Giles. "Arabella is a delightful child and she is one of the most beautiful females I have yet to meet. But I am old enough to be her—well, her much older brother, and I am certain she regards me in that light."

"Do not misunderstand me, Giles," said his mother. "If, after Arabella has had the opportunity to meet other young men of the *ton,* she decides, as I believe she will, that an older man of experience and address suits her, I shall be delighted. She is prettily behaved, of good family, and she will have a comfortable settlement. I do not wish the gossip-mongers to say that I held Arabella back, intending her for you all the time."

"This is absurd," said Giles impatiently. "Arabella is not in love with me nor I with her. If anyone objects to my entertaining my mother's goddaughter—who also happens to be a guest in our house—well, I have no patience for the petty gossiping of busybodies. And now, if you will excuse me . . ." He turned and walked out of the room.

"Giles!" said his mother sharply. He did not answer and she heard his footsteps as he strode down the stairs. "He was always the most stubborn child," she said aloud. "So unlike his brother." Her thoughts dwelled on her elder, more compliant son, and then returned to her immediate problem. "I certainly hope the doctor gives him leave to return to duty shortly," she said. "I must remember to speak to him about it."

When Giles returned home that afternoon, he found Arabella waiting for him. She was wearing a dark blue velvet suit trimmed with fur, and her blue eyes sparkled as she smiled at him.

"This time I am ready and you are late!" she said with a giggle.

"But I knew that if I came home late you would have time to arrange your hair or select a more fetching bonnet," said Giles.

"Oh, you are teasing me," said Arabella.

"Only a little," said Giles with a smile. "Shall we go?"

"Yes, please," said Arabella. They walked to the carriage, which was waiting in front of the house, and Giles helped Arabella inside. They joined the parade of clattering carriages along the cobbled streets of Mayfair until they reached the Park at the fashionable hour when members of the *ton* went to see and be seen. Giles pointed out the Duke of Dorset on his white horse, the Earl of Sefton and the Ladies Molyneux, the Regent himself and the reigning Beauties; among them the Duchesses of Rutland and Argyll and Ladies Cowper and Mountjoy. The ladies vied with each other, not only in the elegance of their dress, but in the appointments and upholstery of their carriages and the liveries of their powdered-wigged footmen. It was a heady feeling for Arabella to be part of Society.

"So many elegant ladies!" she exclaimed.

"They are probably very envious of you," said Giles.

"Of me!" exclaimed Arabella. "Why should such beautiful ladies be jealous of me?"

"Their beauty comes from hours of preparation while yours comes from youth and nature."

Arabella looked at Giles through her long lashes, saying nothing. Suddenly her attention was diverted by a carriage stopping alongside theirs.

"Mr. Kendal," said a voice from the other carriage.

"Miss Chessington," said Giles. "How nice to see you again." Eyeing her companion, he said coolly, "And you, Bradford."

"Kendal," replied Adrian.

There was a silence, which Caroline broke.

"I am sorry we have not been introduced," she said to Arabella. "I am Caroline Chessington."

"Oh, excuse me," said Giles. "I forget my duties. Miss Chessington, Mr. Bradford, may I present my mother's goddaughter, Arabella Chedworth, who is here for her first Season. Arabella, Miss Chessington is also a newcomer to London."

"How do you do?" said Arabella shyly.

"How lovely to meet you, Miss Chedworth," said Caroline. "You must be very excited about the Season. I am certain yours will be a very successful one."

"Thank you," said Arabella. "Everyone has been so kind to me, so very kind. Will I see you at any of the parties?"

"No, I shouldn't think so," said Caroline. "I live a quiet life and my stay in London is only for a short time."

"But London is so exciting!" said Arabella ingenuously as everyone smiled. "So much to do and see. I could not see it all if I stayed a lifetime. So many balls and Assemblies. I am even to have a ball just in my honor."

Caroline smiled. "It does sound exciting for you. But I am happy with my more quiet enjoyments."

"And I am shamed to admit that I have been monopolizing Miss Chessington's time of late to the exclusion of other pleasures," Adrian added smoothly.

"I think we must be getting on," said Giles, clearly peeved at Bradford's proprietary air. "Miss Chessington, your obedient. Bradford . . ." He bowed, but before the carriages could move on in opposite directions, Arabella turned to Giles and said, "I should like it above all things if Miss Chessington and Mr. Bradford could come to my ball." She looked at Caroline, adding, "It will be the grandest party. You would not wish to miss it and I should love to have you there." She looked around triumphantly, unaware that she had discomfited both Giles and Caroline. Giles glowered, Caroline looked nonplussed, while Adrian smiled smugly, enjoying Kendal's embarrassment.

Caroline spoke first. "That is very kind of you, Miss Chedworth," she began, "but I do not think . . ."

"I am certain Miss Chessington would find your ball not to her liking," said Giles, interrupting.

"But on the contrary, I should be delighted to attend, Miss Chedworth," said Caroline, shooting Giles a challenging look. How dare he presume to speak for her! It was not enough that he had voiced his disapproval of Adrian Bradford's attentions, or that his own attentions to her had diminished, but here he was, making a cake of himself over a child just out of the schoolroom!

"And so shall I," added Adrian Bradford, completing Giles's discomfiture.

"Splendid!" said Arabella with a happy smile. "I do so want everyone to share in my good fortune."

"I think we really must be getting on," said Giles stiffly, for there seemed to be nothing more to be said. For the second time, he bade them good day and the carriages moved on.

When they were safely out of earshot, Adrian looked at Caroline quizzically.

"Do you indeed mean to honor that silly child's invitation?"

"Of course not," said Caroline. "It would be most improper. What would her mama say? I am sorry I permitted myself to be goaded."

"It would seem that your friend Mr. Kendal has established himself successfully," said Adrian.

"Miss Chedworth is charming," said Caroline.

"It would not be at all surprising if a betrothal were announced before she had time to test the waters, as it were," said Adrian.

"Giles Kendal and that child?" exclaimed Caroline, annoyed at hearing her feelings voiced. "I thought his attitude was quite avuncular."

"Perhaps," said Adrian. "One could scarcely expect him to make his attentions known before Miss Chedworth is out."

"I am certain Mr. Kendal's affairs are no concern of mine," said Caroline sharply. "Tell me, did you really enjoy the play last night? I am afraid I thought it insipid."

"I did as well," said Adrian, "but as I suggested it and you and Miss Peakirk seemed to enjoy it, I hid my feelings. Now it seems the joke is on me! I should have been honest with you."

"I hope you always will be," said Caroline as they drove on.

"Do you know Miss Chessington well?" asked Arabella as they continued around the Park.

"No, not very well," said Giles in a preoccupied tone.

"I hope you did not mind that I invited her to my ball. I thought she was a friend of yours and I did it to please you. Was it improper of me? I hope you are not angry. Mama often tells me to think before I speak and I am afraid I did not."

"No, of course I'm not angry," said Giles. "And if your mama agrees, it is perfectly all right to send them invitations. Miss Chessington's chaperone should also be included."

"She seems so self-confident," said Arabella. "And on such good terms with Mr. Bradford."

"Yes, so she did," said Giles. "She didn't listen to me," he mused.

"What do you mean?" asked Arabella.

"Nothing," said Giles. "Nothing at all."

"Giles?" asked Arabella diffidently.

"Yes, Arabella," he replied.

"Have I said something to displease you?" she asked. "You're so quiet."

"No, you've not," said Giles. "It's not you at all." He smiled at her. "If we don't return home soon, Mama will be quite displeased and deny us tea."

Arabella's laughter tinkled. "Dear Aunt Henrietta! Oh, she could never be so unkind. But indeed we should not be late. I would not wish to appear rude."

"You never like to hurt anyone, do you?" asked Giles.

"How could I when everyone is so nice to me?" asked Arabella.

To that Giles ventured no reply.

When Giles and Arabella drove up to the house, they found a carriage being unloaded.

"Mama!" exclaimed Arabella. "Mama is here!" She quickly stepped down from the carriage and ran into the house. Lady Kimborough met her as she entered.

"Dear Arabella, such a lovely surprise. Your mama has arrived."

"Oh, where is she? Tell me, please!"

"Here I am, my love," said Mrs. Chedworth, coming into the hallway. A woman of middle years, she was still handsome, and it was easy to see from whom Arabella had inherited her good looks. Her blond hair might have a touch of gray, but her figure was still good and she carried herself as if she, too, were in her first Season.

"Oh, Mama, I have missed you so. Dear Aunt Henrietta and Giles, too, have been so wonderful, but it is not at all the same thing as having one's own mama here. And the children: Are they all well at last? And dear Papa?"

"Hush, my dear, you are much too excited. It is not at all becoming to appear too obviously pleased. The children are all recovering; your papa has left to go on some business or other and he will join us in a few days. It was time for me to be here with you. I have engaged a house for your ball, but it is not yet ready; whilst I had intended to remove us to Pulteney's Hotel, dear Henrietta has prevailed upon me to stay here until it is ready."

"You will love it here, Mama," said Arabella. "I do. Giles has taken me for rides in the Park and he has given me such a pretty fan to go with my gown. Let me show it to you." She ran out of the room.

Mrs. Chedworth raised her eyebrows. "Arabella seems very happy, Henrietta," she said. "I knew that I could rely on you. But tell me, I hope that Giles has not bored himself entertaining a child just out of the schoolroom. I would not want Arabella to be a nuisance to him."

"I am sure she is not that," said Lady Kimborough. "Such a sweet child; so engaging, so charming. I am certain Giles has enjoyed having her here to bear him company. She, I know, regards him as an elder brother or a doting uncle."

"Indeed," said Mrs. Chedworth carefully. "I am delighted to know that Arabella has found such a friend. An elder brother can be such a help in one's first Season. Naturally," she continued, "I wish Arabella to meet many eligible gentlemen. Neither her father nor myself wish her to fix her affections before she has had the opportunity to 'spread her wings,' as they say. I do not scruple to tell you, Henrietta, that the cost of presenting a daughter is higher than we had thought, and there are the other girls to consider and none of them the beauty Arabella is. Chedworth has even been thinking of selling out of the Funds! We are no longer in the position of being able to permit Arabella to pick and choose without regard to fortune."

"I understand," said Lady Kimborough. "I should like nothing better than for the dear child to make a splendid match, which I predict that she shall. Tell me, when did you say your house will be ready? I dread the thought of losing Arabella, but I know you must wish to be established under your own roof."

At that moment, Arabella returned to the room, bearing the fan.

"See, Mama, isn't it lovely?"

"Very nice, my love. It was very kind of Giles to give you such a gift; as if he were the older brother you never had."

Arabella contemplated that. "But Giles is not . . ." She blushed fiercely. "I think I must change," she said. She curtsied slightly and excused herself.

"Perhaps it will be best that we establish ourselves under our own roof as quickly as possible. I am certain you understand." Her eyes met Lady Kimborough's and there was a challenge in them. But there was something more. There was concern as well.

CHAPTER 11

Mrs. Chedworth was as good as her word. Within a week of her arrival the house had been readied and she had removed herself and Arabella to it. Mr. Chedworth's arrival several days later to carry out his obligations during his daughter's come-out completed the removal of Arabella from the Kimborough sphere. On the night of the ball being held in Arabella's honor, Lady Kimborough commented on it to her husband when he entered her boudoir. She signaled to her maid to leave and said, "You know, Kimborough, I have scarcely seen Arabella since she left here."

"As I understood it, my love, you did not wish it to appear as if you were monopolizing Arabella's attention or trying to marry her to Giles. Have not things worked out exactly as you planned?"

"Whilst I did not wish Giles to appear to monopolize Arabella, I certainly did not expect Lavinia to so completely isolate her. I do not believe Giles has seen her once! And I do not credit Lavinia's cry of poverty. I am most displeased with her. I am one of her oldest friends. I believe she does not wish Arabella to marry Giles. And he is not exactly nobody! He is the son of an earl and of an earl's daughter, after all! She should consider herself fortunate to be able to marry her daughter to a Kendal!"

"Giles shall certainly have the opportunity to see her tonight, my love," said Kimborough mildly. "From what I have heard at the clubs, the entire world has been invited this evening. Your protégée's reputation has preceded her and she is certain to be one of the catches of the Season. If Chedworth's fortune has diminished, it is not generally known. Giles had better take care. He would not wish to lose the opportunity to marry a female of beauty and fortune, but he would also not wish to find himself leg-shackled to a female whose fortune has disappeared. I do know that it would be of no use to speak to Giles. He'll make up his own mind."

"It is regrettable, Kimborough, that Giles need take after your family. There is a stubbornness about him which puts me rather painfully in mind of your father." She picked up her fan. "Shall we go?"

"Yes, my love," replied her lord meekly.

In Woburn Square, Caroline was also dressing for the ball. She had been surprised and not a little chagrined to receive an invitation for herself and Aurelia. She knew that it had been at Giles Kendal's prompting and presumed he had done it to show her that he was generosity itself. For her part, she had not the least desire to watch Giles Kendal make a fool of himself over Arabella Chedworth, but she did not want him to think that she had cried craven. She had vowed to look her best and she was indeed in fine looks. Her gown, in the ashes-of-roses pink that was so becoming to her, was shot through with silver thread. The bodice and small puffed sleeves were edged with deeper pink ruching, as was the ruffle at the bottom of the skirt. Her shoes were of the same deep pink silk. Around her neck was a strand of pearls and another strand was interwoven with pink ribbon through her hair. If she had fears about the success of her costume, the doubts were dispelled by the arrival of Adrian Bradford to escort them to the ball.

"My dear Miss Chessington," he said as she descended the staircase to meet him. "You are enchanting!"

"Thank you, kind sir," said Caroline, extending her hand playfully. "And may I say that you are most truly the gentleman."

Adrian bowed. He was wearing full evening dress, with his chapeau-bras correctly folded under his arm.

As they spoke, Aurelia came into the room. She was nursing a bad cold and was despondent that she was forced to miss such a fashionable ball.

"Are you quite certain, my love, that I should not make an effort to accompany you? I am afraid it is not at all the thing for you to go alone. People will think you are fast." She sneezed.

"Nonsense, Aurelia," said Caroline, kissing her. "It is not my first Season, you know. Besides, who will know me?"

"I shall take excellent care of Miss Chessington," said Adrian, "although I deeply regret being able to escort only one of the belles of the evening."

Thus cajoled and reassured, Aurelia tottered back to bed. Caroline was guiltily conscious of a feeling of relief.

When the Kimborough carriage arrived in Berkeley Square, guests were already alighting and the house was aglow with lights. They were greeted by Lavinia Chedworth, gowned in exquisite taste in shot-purple gauze over satin, trimmed with gold and enhanced by the Chedworth amethysts. But there was no doubt in whose honor the ball was given. Arabella, her color heightened by the occasion, looked enchanting. Her mama had wisely limited her accessories to a garland of white flowers in her hair, a pearl necklace, and Giles's fan. She greeted the Kimboroughs prettily

"Ah, dearest Godmama and Lord Kimborough. It has been such a long time but you must forgive me! I have been so busy. I had no idea that having a Season involved so much preparation. You must think me a perfect wretch for having neglected you."

Lord Kimborough beamed and said that the wait was certainly worth the opportunity to see her in such looks.

"Kimborough," said his lady reprovingly, "would you fetch me some punch?"

"Yes, my love," said Lord Kimborough. "Now you save a dance for me, you saucy puss," he remarked as he strode off.

"Indeed, Arabella, you are looking lovely," said Lady Kimborough when her husband had gone. "But I am sorry we have not seen you. I had thought perhaps your mama would have wished the benefit . . ."

"Of what, Mama?" asked a voice behind her.

"Giles!" exclaimed Arabella with pleasure. "How wonderful to see you!"

Lady Kimborough, not at all pleased at being interrupted, was nevertheless delighted to see the pleasure with which her son was greeted.

"I do not believe you have missed me at all," he teased. "You are surrounded by so many other admirers."

Lady Kimborough stepped away as Arabella blushed fiercely. Just then a young buck, an aspiring Dandy sporting extremely high points on his collar, wide lapels, and a waterfall knot in his cravat, came up and bowed. "I believe the next dance is mine, Miss Chedworth," he said. "Evening, Kendal."

"Will you excuse me, Giles?" she asked.

"Of course," he said. "Enjoy it. But save one for me."

"I shall," said Arabella as she danced away.

Giles, not wishing to dance with anyone else, strolled to the entrance hall just in time to see Caroline sail in on Adrian Bradford's arm. He felt a jolt of surprise. Giles had not really thought Caroline would come, although she had accepted Arabella's invitation. She looked elegant, he thought, and her presence disturbed him, but he was not sure why. He really did not know Caroline Chessington, despite the several times they had been together. He had been caught up in squiring Arabella Chedworth through the first weeks of her first Season; now he was sorry that his acquaintance with Caroline Chessington had languished. He had enjoyed their conversation, he recalled. Then Arabella had arrived and the next thing he had known, Caroline was constantly in Adrian Bradford's company. Each time he and Caroline had met after that, they had been at cross-purposes—all because of her stubbornness, he thought grimly. Well, he would show her how magnanimous he could be.

As he approached the party, Caroline smiled in welcome.

"Miss Chessington," he said. "I am delighted to see you. You are looking lovely. Bradford." He bowed.

"Mr. Kendal," said Caroline. "Such a lovely party. And Miss Chedworth is in such enchanting looks."

"Miss Chessington," said Adrian, "I believe you have promised me the first dance."

"Indeed I have," said Caroline. "Will you excuse us?"

For the second time, Giles felt rebuffed.

"May I claim another dance and the honor of escorting you into supper?" he asked.

"Miss Chessington will be accompanying me," said Adrian.

"I believe Miss Chessington can speak for herself," said Giles evenly.

Caroline, who had come prepared to be distant to Giles, was now annoyed at Adrian's high-handed tactics.

"I should be delighted to dine with you, Mr. Kendal," she said. "And now, Mr. Bradford, I believe this dance is ours."

Arabella was, in fact, able to give Giles only one dance, for she was never without a partner. She would not dance with any of her admirers more than twice, and neither the importunings of Mr. Geoffrey Stanhope that she was the embodiment of a goddess nor the insistent requests made by the odious Lord Warriner, who seemed quite old and fat, were enough to change her resolution. Her mama had told her she must on no account encourage one gentleman over another at her come-out, and she would not dream of disobeying her mama. Such a wonderful ball! And

Mama and Papa so concerned about her happiness! No, she would never disobey Mama.

She did wish she had been able to talk to Mr. Jeremy Tarkington more. From the moment he'd been introduced to her by Mr. Farnham she'd been attracted to him. He had brought her some punch and they'd spoken briefly. He was a poet, although he said his family, stodgy and traditional, did not consider that a suitable occupation for the son of a viscount. They were forcing him to go to Cambridge to study for a political career or some other gentlemanly occupation as yet undetermined, and he was home only on holiday. As for Arabella, she thought being a poet was the very thing! It was so romantic! And he was so handsome. Just the way a young man should look, with his brooding eyes and melancholy smile. He'd promised to compose a poem about the way she looked tonight. He'd said a poet had to search for such inspiration as she provided. Arabella could not wait to receive it. No one had ever written a poem about her before. What a wonderful night it was!

After a sumptuous supper consisting of roast beef, mutton, fillet of veal, Perigord pies, truffles, several removes, jellies, and an array of pastries, fruits, and sweetmeats accompanied by champagne, Giles and Caroline found themselves alone on a terrace.

"Are you enjoying yourself, Miss Chessington?" he asked.

"Oh, yes," said Caroline.

"You are attracting some attention," said Giles. "Several people have asked me who you are."

"I hope you told them no one of importance," said Caroline.

"I said I wasn't certain I knew," said Giles. "I would like to know much better." He took her hands gently in his and tenderly brought them to his lips. Then, holding both her hands in his, as though reluctant to relinquish them, he continued, "Miss Chessington . . . Caroline . . . I hope . . ." He paused.

Caroline gazed up at him. His face seemed different: softer, less guarded. His eyes held a warmth, a look almost of entreaty.

He drew her closer and she felt him put his arms around her, his head bending to meet hers. Their lips met fleetingly, softly. As they drew apart, Giles began again, "Caroline, my dear . . ." Just then a voice from behind him said mockingly, "I believe you have promised this dance to me." It was Adrian Bradford, and Giles swore under his breath.

"Oh," said Caroline breathlessly, for it was a new sensation, being sought after by two men. She found that she liked it. She turned to Giles.

"I did promise this dance to Mr. Bradford," she said. In an effort to offend neither suitor, she sounded colder and more distant than she had intended. Giles Kendal colored, nodded politely, and watched them as they left for the ballroom.

He carefully avoided Caroline for the rest of the evening, instead standing aside and watching Arabella in her triumphant come-out. He was unaware that Caroline was carefully watchful of him and of the attention he was directing toward Arabella. She was puzzled, first by his actions on the terrace, and then by his apparent lack of interest. Was he playing a game with her emotions? Was it jealousy, or dislike of Adrian Bradford? For a moment, she had felt something real between them. It could not be that Giles was merely flirting with her. That was not his way, and he had been too sincere, too tender, too loving, to have been engaging in a flirtation.

Caroline, preoccupied with her thoughts, did not realize that she was attracting attention herself. Adrian had discovered that, too. During supper, some of his erstwhile friends, knowing that he was hanging out for a rich wife, had twitted him about his unknown companion and his attentiveness to her.

"Must be plump in the pocket," one had commented, "or Adrian's lost his touch." Bradford had smiled cynically at this and replied, "Family obligation—the daughter of a distant, rather provincial cousin to whom, regrettably, I find myself in debt. I offered to show her London. Her first trip, you know." He hoped that would dispel gossip, for he did not wish to encourage any further interest in Miss Caroline Chessington and he especially did not want anyone to know that the object of his attentions was an heiress. He did not need competition.

Lady Kimborough, too, had noticed Caroline and Giles's interest in her. When she asked Giles about his elegant supper companion, his explanation that she was a visitor from the North who lived in Woburn Square with an elderly relation satisfied her that he was in no danger from that source.

CHAPTER 12

The next morning the doorbell rang constantly in Berkeley Square. Reade, the butler, was kept busy answering it and receiving the stream of flowers, notes, and callers come to see the lovely Miss Chedworth again. Reade accepted the gifts and told the visitors that Miss Chedworth was not receiving today. He had been given strict orders by his mistress to admit no one, for Miss Chedworth needed to rest after her very late night. Actually, she was concerned that Arabella looked a trifle pale, and she did not wish to dispel the vision already created. To do so, she told Arabella, would be fatal.

"But, Mama," Arabella protested, "am I not to see any of the gentlemen? Look at the lovely note from Mr. Stanhope which he sent with these violets." She handed the note to her mother, who scanned it quickly.

"It will not do to encourage Mr. Stanhope at this time, my love," said Mrs. Chedworth. "You would not wish to fix your affections so quickly."

"But how long must I wait before I fix my affections, Mama?" asked Arabella.

"To favor one gentleman over another so quickly would arouse comment, my love. You might even be denied entrance to Almack's! After you have had time to meet other gentlemen will be the time to fix your affections on one. You still have routs and parties to go to, my love. The Season has just begun!"

There was a knock at the door.

"Come in," said Mrs. Chedworth. Reade opened the door.

"If you please, madam, there is a young gentleman downstairs who is most insistent about seeing Miss Chedworth."

"Have you told him Miss Chedworth is not receiving visitors today?"

"Naturally, madam, I have followed your instructions. Mr. Tarkington, however, insists that he must see Miss Chedworth. I thought it better to inform you."

At the mention of Mr. Tarkington, Arabella had looked up. "Oh, Mama, mayn't I see Mr. Tarkington?" she asked.

Mrs. Chedworth cast a puzzled look at her daughter.

"You did right in informing me of the situation, Reade," she said to the butler. "I shall come downstairs and speak to Mr. Tarkington myself."

"Very good, madam," said Reade. He closed the door as he left.

"Oh, Mama, please let me see Mr. Tarkington," pleaded Arabella. "He said he would . . . I most particularly wish to speak to him."

Mrs. Chedworth looked at her daughter sharply.

"It would be most improper to receive Mr. Tarkington after we have denied persons of greater consequence and said you were not well. Why are you so eager to see him? You scarcely spoke to him last night."

"He—Mr. Tarkington—seemed most pleasant." She did not want to tell her mother about Jeremy's poetry, because she felt her mother would react as Jeremy's parents had. "I would just like to see him again, for I believe he will be returning to school soon."

"That may be," said Mrs. Chedworth, "but it would still be inappropriate to see him. I shall explain the situation to Mr. Tarkington." She stood up. "I shall have some hot chocolate sent up to you," she said. "You should rest."

"Yes, Mama," said Arabella. Her mother did not miss the tone of regret in her daughter's voice. She had better see to Mr. Tarkington. If Arabella had conceived a *tendre* for a schoolboy, she would have to put a stop to it; gently, but certainly. As she entered the morning room she saw an extremely handsome young man standing there.

"Mr. Tarkington?" she said.

"Yes, ma'am," he replied, somewhat uncomfortably.

"You must forgive me for not being able to speak with you last night. I understand that you have come to see my daughter. That is very thoughtful of you, but I am sorry to say that she is unable to see you. She is feeling not quite the thing, as Reade explained to you."

"I know, ma'am, but I was hoping—that is, I have something I wish to give to Miss Chedworth."

"I shall be happy to accept it for you," said Mrs. Chedworth.

Too well-bred to explain that he would rather give them to Arabella himself, Jeremy was forced to hand the flowers and note he carried to Mrs. Chedworth.

"And now, if you will excuse me, Mr. Tarkington, I must have some chocolate sent up to Arabella. It was very kind of you to call."

There was nothing for Jeremy to do. He made his bow to Mrs. Chedworth and left without waiting to be shown to the door.

Mrs. Chedworth pondered the envelope in her hand. She could not withhold it from Arabella, because if Arabella met Mr. Tarkington again, he might refer to it. She would have to give it to her, but she would do what she could to neutralize its effect. She could see why Arabella, young and impressionable, would be charmed by such a tall, handsome young man. But he was still a schoolboy. She'd have to find out more about his family, but there was no reason to think he'd be an acceptable match. Arabella would no doubt outgrow her infatuation. Mrs. Chedworth would be happy, she thought with a sigh, when Arabella was safely married to the proper person.

Arabella had been very disappointed at not seeing Jeremy, but when her mother handed her the note and flowers from him, her disappointment vanished.

"Did Mr. Tarkington leave a message for me?" she asked.

"No, my love, he just requested that I give you these. I don't know why he could not give them to Reade as all the other gentlemen did. That is probably the result of his youth. Were he older, he would not be quite so impetuous."

Arabella was only partially listening. She trembled as she opened the envelope. There was indeed a poem inside. She did not wish to read it with her mother present.

"Mama," she said diffidently, "could I be alone for a while?"

"Of course, my love," said her mother, not at all pleased. Thinking quickly, she said, "If you're rested this afternoon, perhaps you would like to go for a ride in the Park."

"That would be nice, Mama," said Arabella. Perhaps, she thought, she would see Jeremy if she went to the Park.

"I shall see you later, then," said her mother as she closed the door.

Arabella barely waited until her mother had gone before she turned to the poem in her hand.

To Venus

When first I beheld you last night
a vision arising as from a dream,
I was swept aside by the thought
of a Paradise as yet unseen.

Her eyes moistened and she could read no further than the first few lines. It was so lovely, and it was about her. She could hardly believe it. She had to see Jeremy again to thank him. She had to find a way.

CHAPTER 13

On the same afternoon, Giles decided to call on Caroline again. He was torn by the conflicting desire to resume his acquaintance with her and the unpleasant thought that he really must warn Caroline that she was becoming a subject for the gossip-mongers.

Even before Arabella's ball, he had heard conversation of a Miss Chessington who was seen frequently with Adrian Bradford. No one seemed to know anything about her except that she lived in Woburn Square with an elderly companion. As there was no indication of great fortune, no one could understand why Adrian Bradford was making her the object of his attentions. The further speculation he had overheard the previous evening had convinced him of the need to inform her of the situation. It was not a task he relished.

When he was ushered into Caroline's parlor, he found the task would be even more difficult than he'd imagined. Sitting with Caroline was Adrian Bradford.

Giles was too well-bred to allow his discomfiture to show, and he responded to Caroline's greeting courteously. He found himself perversely irritated with Caroline upon finding Adrian present, because it both confirmed the necessity for the errand and made it impossible to carry out. How obtuse of her not to see what a false fellow he was! He'd thought her a woman of sense, but if she could not tell a bounder from a gentleman, she was no more than a peagoose.

"Mr. Kendal?" Caroline was saying. Giles returned to the conversation. "Mr. Bradford was saying that Miss Chedworth seems to have taken the *ton* by storm."

"Yes," replied Giles mechanically, "she has." Damn his impudence! Giles thought. It is not enough that he need make Caroline a source of conversation for the gossip-mongers. If he trifles with Arabella, I swear I'll call him out! He stood up.

"I am afraid I must be going," he said.

"So soon?" asked Adrian Bradford, a touch of malice in his voice.

"I am afraid so," said Giles. "Miss Chessington, I should like to speak to you privately about a matter of some importance. May I call tomorrow?"

"Yes, of course," said Caroline. "I shall be at home and alone in the morning. I shall be pleased to see you then."

"Until tomorrow, then," said Giles, making his bow. He barely acknowledged Adrian as he left the room.

"Well!" said Adrian. "I fear your protector was none too pleased to find me here. Though why it should be a concern of his I'm sure I don't know, since the *on dit* is that the Kimboroughs have him slated for the fair Arabella."

"I don't know what you are talking about," said Caroline stiffly. "Mr. Kendal is most certainly not my protector, and I am certain he can have no interest or concern in whom I choose to have as my guest." Then, spoiling the effect of her words, she added, "And his romantic affairs are certainly no concern of mine!"

When Adrian merely raised an eyebrow in cool amusement, she went on, "I think his discomfort was the result of his not finding me alone when he wished to talk privately. I am certain he would have felt the same way had my cousin been present."

"Perhaps," said Adrian skeptically. "What do you think he has to say to you which is of such a private nature?"

"I have no idea," said Caroline.

"Perhaps he wished to warn you about me," said Adrian playfully.

"That's nonsense," replied Caroline sharply. "I do not need his judgment. Do you not think we've spent quite enough time wondering about Mr. Kendal?"

"Yes, indeed," said Adrian, taking his cue from her. They chatted for a few moments more on inconsequential topics and then Adrian took his leave.

It may be time for me to show my hand, he thought as he walked down the street.

For her part, Caroline was exceedingly angry. She had told Adrian that she did not know why Giles wanted to speak to her, but that was not completely true. It had not taken her long to discern that Giles Kendal did not like Adrian Bradford. Their personalities were too different for either to feel comfortable with the other. But if Giles were to use his dislike as the basis for a warning about Adrian, it would be the outside of enough! She would not tolerate any such interference in her personal affairs. Certainly not from someone such as Giles Kendal, who seemed to be smitten by a child distinguished by more beauty than brains. She'd thought him a man of superior sense, but anyone who would be infatuated by a silly widgeon such as Arabella Chedworth was not in a position to give advice to anyone else.

Caroline was therefore in a dangerous mood when Giles came to call the next morning. Had he known her better he would have recognized this from the hard gleam in her eyes. Aurelia, who had teased her at breakfast over her "many conquests" had discovered that Caroline was in no mood to be teased.

She greeted Giles in the parlor, speaking rather formally.

"I am sorry that it was necessary for you to make a special visit here," she said as she bade him to be seated.

"It was no trouble at all," Giles replied.

There was a silence.

"Pray tell me the object of this visit," said Caroline.

"The errand is not an easy one, Miss Chessington," said Giles. "I trust you will not misinterpret my intentions."

"I wish you will state your intention," said Caroline. "So far I have had little to misinterpret."

"All right, then," said Giles, plunging in. "I have heard comments about your relationship with Adrian Bradford. People wonder about the 'mysterious' Miss Chessington. Your frequent appearances with him have attracted attention which I am certain you do not desire. Perhaps this sounds harsh, but Adrian Bradford cannot add to your consequence. You know that."

"I beg you go no further," said Caroline. "You have no right to censure my conduct. If gossip-mongers have nothing else to do but wonder about me, then London is flat indeed! And if Mr. Bradford is, indeed, a fortune hunter, it should surprise everyone that he is seen in my company. If it were thought that I had a fortune, that, too, would be food for the gossip-mongers!"

"I do not know why Adrian Bradford has attached himself to you . . ." began Giles clumsily.

"Naturally not," said Caroline icily. "We have established that I have no fortune, and you have made it clear that there is no other reason for anyone to show a preference for me. It is clear that you do not. It is apparent that you prefer someone of sweet but insipid demeanor."

"Just what do you mean by that, Miss Chessington?" he asked.

"Merely that I believe our tastes to be quite different," she replied.

"My taste is not setting the *ton* on its ears!" said Giles angrily.

"Of course not," agreed Caroline. "When a man chooses to make a fool of himself over a child, no one considers it improper."

"I am not making a fool of myself!" shouted Giles.

"Then you are not listening to yourself," replied Caroline

sweetly. She stood up. "I do not think there is anything further for us to discuss, Mr. Kendal," she said. "I do not wish to appear rude, but I have an engagement this afternoon and I must change my gown."

"Had I believed that my concern would be so amusing to you, I should not have bothered to come here," said Giles coldly. "I came because I thought myself your friend; because I cared what happened to you. I shall not disturb you again. Please accept my apologies and my best wishes for your future." He strode out of the room.

"Oh!" said Caroline, clenching her fists. "How could I have let him leave while he had the last word!"

Caroline was so enraged at Giles's interference that she was unable to keep the details from Adrian. He listened soberly.

"I am not surprised at Kendal's feelings," he said when she had finished her tale. "I have never been a favorite of his; despite our fathers' acquaintanceship, he has never liked me. It is true that I have a reputation as a fortune hunter; it is easy to despise fortune hunters when you yourself have no need to be one. Kendal may be a younger son, but his prospects in the Diplomatic are good. He was fortunate in having Lord Walsingham to sponsor him. I was not so fortunate."

"Indeed, I have often noticed that rank may substitute for fortune and fortune for rank," replied Caroline warmly.

"I began by saying that I have a reputation as a fortune hunter, and that is true to an extent. It is also true that the only way for me to restore my name would be to regain the fortune which my father and uncles lost."

"Then why . . ." Caroline paused and reddened. "Then why . . ."

". . . do I seek out your company when you have no fortune?" finished Adrian.

"Yes, that's it," said Caroline, turning away.

"I find that you, my dear Caroline, have something more lasting than fortune. Your spirit, your vitality, make me feel that somehow I can succeed and restore my family name in some other way. I had not meant to speak, but I cannot permit Kendal to poison your mind against me!"

"I am not so suggestible," said Caroline.

"No, but if I thought that you doubted my motives in coming to see you . . . forgive me. I do not wish to embarrass you, and I have no right to speak. You know my situation; it would be unfair to you."

"Why is it that men feel they must make decisions for me? I can decide what is best for me!"

"But surely you can understand my reluctance to leave you open to the comments of those whose acceptance you would desire."

"I am past the age of caring what others think."

"But if you stayed in London, you would soon wish to be a part of the fashionable world."

"Thus far I have managed to avoid the temptation."

"Ah, but you have not been long in London! Were you a resident, you would crave the balls, the routs, the promenades in the Park."

"Will you believe me when I say that I would not!" Caroline exclaimed impatiently. She took a turn around the room. "I would not spend all my time in London," she said. "I would like to return to—to my home in Lancashire, for I would not wish to be away from there too long. You see," she said with a smile, "I am a country girl at heart and would soon feel out of place in London."

Adrian looked sober. "If I could believe that to be true . . ." he said.

"It is true!" she cried. "What must I do to make you believe me? Has Giles Kendal convinced even you that he is right? If I refuse to accept his notions of propriety, then you should do the same."

Adrian walked to her and took her hand. "I must think," he said. "There is so much to say, but I must be alone to think. In your presence, it is impossible for me to think rationally." He kissed her hand and strode out of the room.

Caroline, her cheeks burning brightly, pressed the hand he had kissed to her face. She knew she should be feeling happiness, but what she felt was confusion.

"What have I done?" she wondered aloud. "What have I done?"

Giles, for his part, left Woburn Square in a rage such as he had rarely known. He felt contempt for Adrian Bradford, but his rage was reserved for Caroline Chessington, for being stubborn, arrogant, sarcastic, and for putting him in the position of making a fool of himself. That he had initiated the exchange he did not consider: he had done it for her own good, and all he had to show for his concern was humiliation! Who did she think she was, this Caroline Chessington? How could he have felt drawn to her? Why did he still feel so? If she weren't careful, she'd find herself married to Adrian Bradford and all his debts. The one thing he could not understand was why Bradford continued to court Caroline. There was something wrong there. Bradford needed money desperately. That was a puzzle. He couldn't understand that at all.

CHAPTER 14

For several days, Arabella waited for Jeremy to return. He did not come, although Lord Warriner was a frequent visitor. A widower of some forty years, Lord Warriner was wealthy enough to meet with the approbation of the Chedworths. Unfortunately for his chances with Arabella, he was also portly and balding and frequently smelled of wine. He smiled knowingly at Arabella, patted her hand, and said she made him feel young again. Arabella always smiled politely, but she could not like it. He was neither romantic nor handsome, and Arabella could not imagine him writing a poem. She wished he would not come again.

A week after her come-out, on a morning when no one had called, she decided to go shopping with her maid. They were just starting out the door when Jeremy Tarkington appeared, to Arabella's delight. She looked at him and thought, "How much like a poet he is," although if one had asked her what that was, she could not have said. He certainly cut a romantic figure to an impressionable young female, with his dark, disheveled locks carefully arranged à la Byron, his cravat artfully draped, and an air of carefully cultivated languor which belied his pleasure at seeing her.

"You've come back!" she exclaimed. "I knew you would." Maria, her maid, walked discreetly ahead.

"I wanted to come the very next day, but my father wished me to accompany him to Buckinghamshire. I had no choice! How can I, totally dependent upon them, refuse to do as they say, even as I wish for nothing but to see you again," he declaimed as he artfully struck a pose, being careful not to disturb his appearance.

Arabella blushed fiercely. "I cannot talk now, for the carriage is waiting," she said. "Tomorrow, I shall walk in the Park with Maria at eleven. Now, I must go!" As she stepped into the carriage, she turned and waved to him.

The wait was interminable for Arabella. How could the time pass so slowly until the next day? During dinner, she looked at the clock so often that her father asked her teasingly if she were expecting someone.

"Oh, no, Papa, whom would I be expecting?"

"Seems to me Lord Warriner is around here a lot," said her father.

"Lord Warriner has been a frequent visitor," said Mrs. Chedworth with a quick glance at her daughter. "He admires Arabella a great deal."

"Mama, Lord Warriner is old enough to be my father," said Arabella. "I do not wish him to admire me."

"Any young lady in her first Season should be honored to have such a man of the world as Lord Warriner show an interest in her," said Mrs. Chedworth reprovingly. "It is quite a feather in your cap, my love. A man of wealth, in the first stare of consequence; a girl would be foolish to abjure such a suitor."

"But I don't want wealth or consequence!" said Arabella, getting up from the table. "I want someone I can love!" She sobbed as she ran from the room.

"I believe your daughter has been reading novels from the lending library, my dear," said Mr. Chedworth.

"Indeed!" said Mrs. Chedworth. "I can tell you, sir, that I did not put such foolishness in her head! It is to be expected that a young girl would not initially be attracted to a man such as Lord Warriner. However, I am certain she will, upon reflection, realize that love has nothing to do with marriage."

"Were the situation different . . ." said Mr. Chedworth. "Had I not suffered such ill luck . . ."

"But we cannot change the facts," said Mrs. Chedworth. "We are desperate, Mr. Chedworth. You know the cost of Arabella's come-out. If it does not result in a wealthy husband, it will have been for nothing. And what of the other girls?"

"Do you think Warriner will offer for Arabella?" asked Mr. Chedworth.

"I am convinced of it," answered his wife.

"But if she is opposed to it . . ." said Mr. Chedworth.

"I am certain that Arabella will do just as she ought," replied Mrs. Chedworth. "This phase will pass. I was concerned, at first, that she had conceived a *tendre* for one of Lord Tarkington's sons. A schoolboy! I have made inquiries, discreet, of course, and have ascertained that he has no expectations. He fancies himself a poet! However, he has not been heard from again, and no doubt Arabella has forgotten him."

"I hope you are right, my dear," said Mr. Chedworth.

Of course, Arabella had not forgotten him. As she lay on her bed, she thought of what it would be like to marry Lord Warriner instead of Jeremy. It was too terrible to think about, and when her mother came in to see how she was, she found her daughter fast asleep in her clothes.

The next morning, Arabella asked her mother if she could go for a walk in the Park with Maria.

"I would like some fresh air, Mama," she said.

"Of course, my love," said Mrs. Chedworth, preoccupied with some fabrics which had just arrived.

Arabella slipped on her pelisse before her mother had a chance to change her mind. She and Maria walked to the Park and found Jeremy waiting at the fountain. Maria, sympathetic to the romantic spirit of her young mistress, walked away. Jeremy led Arabella to a secluded bench and held her hand.

"I had to see you before I returned to Cambridge," he declared.

"I wanted to see you, too," said Arabella. "I wanted to thank you for the poem. It was so beautiful."

"A poet needs inspiration," said Jeremy.

"When must you return to school?" asked Arabella.

"In two days," replied Jeremy.

"Two days!" exclaimed Arabella, in despair. "But we shall have no time together."

"I know," said Jeremy, "but I must return. My father would cut me off, if I did not."

"I care nothing for money!" cried Arabella.

"I, too, care nothing for money," said Jeremy. "It is so sordid. I despise having to accept it from my father. But how else can I continue to write my poems? If I did not accept my allowance, I would be forced to seek employment."

"Oh, no," replied Arabella. "That would be horrid. You must be able to write."

"You do understand," said Jeremy, squeezing her hand. "I knew you would. From the moment I saw you, I knew you had a soul." He pressed her hand to his lips. "Oh, Arabella, we belong together."

Arabella blushed again. "Oh, Jeremy," she whispered. They looked at each other for a moment. Then, Arabella turned away.

"It is so hopeless," she said. "I shall never be allowed to wait until you finish school. I shall be forced to marry Lord Warriner, and I shall be lost to you!"

"Lord Warriner!" exclaimed Jeremy. "Every thought revolts! Why, he is quite old! He cannot be allowed to claim you as his!"

"I know," said Arabella. "But he has a fortune, and that is all that my parents care about. I have nothing to say in the matter."

"If only I had a fortune. I could leave school—defy my parents —and we could be together! Lord Warriner would never have you!"

"If only I were clever. I could sew or teach pianoforte and Italian," said Arabella. "Then, you would not have to work and could spend your time writing."

"How noble of you, to sacrifice yourself for me," said Jeremy. "But, alas, it can never be. I must return to school."

"And I shall never see you again!" cried Arabella. "You will not be able to write to me, for they will see your letters. It is monstrously unfair!" She put her head in her hands and began to weep.

Just then, Maria approached.

"Excuse me, Miss Arabella," she said timidly. "And sir," she added.

"What is it?" asked Arabella, wiping her eyes, for she did not wish them to become too red.

"It is getting late, and the mistress will wonder where you are."

"Then I must go," she replied. She turned to Jeremy. "Please, do not forget me."

"I could not," he answered, kissing her hand again.

Arabella stood up. "Good-bye, then," she said, as she turned away. Behind her Maria followed, dabbing at her eyes.

CHAPTER 15

Several days after his contretemps with Caroline, Giles reported to his family's physician in Harley Street. He'd been feeling so much better, he was certain that he would be able to return to Lord Walsingham soon. Dr. Keene examined him closely, only an occasional "Ah" giving Giles any indication of his findings.

"Well, my boy," he said finally, "you're doing quite well."

"Then, I may return to Vienna?" asked Giles eagerly.

"In due course," said Dr. Keene.

"Due course!" exclaimed Giles. "What the devil does that mean?"

"Don't lose your temper with me, Giles Kendal," said the doctor. "I've known you since you were in short pants. You're a sensible man. You're still quite thin. You don't want to go racketing about and find yourself back in bed. You've had a rough time and a close call, and there's no point in rushing things. After all, it's only been two months. You may consider yourself fortunate it wasn't six. Another month or so, and we'll see. If you like, I'll send a note along to Lord Walsingham with my opinion."

"Thank you, no," replied Giles stiffly. "I'll write to him myself." He began to put on his coat.

"As you wish," said Dr. Keene. "Giles, I know this is a disappointment to you, but, believe me, it is the only prudent course."

"I know, sir," said Giles reluctantly. "I'm sorry I lost my temper with you. I am just eager to return to duty."

"Is London so flat, then?" asked the doctor with a chuckle.

"An unattached young man at the height of the Season: you must be out of sorts if that holds no attraction!"

"Flat it is not," replied Giles. He held out his hand. "Thank you, sir," he said. "I'll see you in a month."

"My compliments to your parents," said the doctor. "By the by, how is your brother's knee? The last time I saw him, he was limping badly."

"It still hurts him quite a bit," replied Giles.

"He was getting a bit thick around the middle," said the doctor. "That won't help the knee. But, then, if patients listened to their doctors, we'd all be out of business." He chuckled again.

"Yes, sir," said Giles with a grin. He left, having almost forgotten that it would be at least a month before he could return to Vienna.

When Giles entered the hallway of his parents' home, he heard the sound of his mother's voice. She was entertaining unidentified guests in the parlor. He tried to escape upstairs unnoticed, but Arabella Chedworth emerged from the parlor before he could get away.

"Oh, I am so glad it is you," she whispered. "I must speak to you, but I cannot do so here. I told Mama and Aunt Henrietta that I thought I had lost my glove so that I could come out here. Can you call tomorrow morning? Mama will be out. I am desperate. Please do not fail me!" She turned and walked back into the room.

"How silly of me," he heard her say. "My glove was in my reticule all the time!"

Giles, slightly stunned by Arabella's speech, continued upstairs. His life, he reflected, was beginning to resemble the novels to which ladies of the *ton* seemed addicted. He had no idea what was troubling Arabella, but he supposed he had better go to see her; otherwise, she might do something foolish.

"And the doctor wondered if London was flat," he said aloud.

"There seems to be more intrigue here than in Vienna." And then, because the whole situation struck him as slightly absurd, he laughed.

The next morning, Giles dutifully presented himself at Berkeley Square. He was greeted by the butler, who recognized his name.

"Miss Chedworth will be down presently," he said as he ushered Giles into the parlor. He had barely nodded and left the room when Arabella hurried in.

"Oh, thank goodness you have come!" she exclaimed. "I am so distressed!" She pulled out a handkerchief and began sobbing.

"My dear Arabella, what has happened? Come, pull yourself together, I cannot help you if you do not tell me what the trouble is!"

Arabella lifted her face from the handkerchief and sniffed. "It is so horrid!" she said.

"What is so horrid?" asked Giles patiently.

"Mama!" Arabella exclaimed.

"Your mama is horrid?" asked Giles, confused.

"No," wailed Arabella. "You don't understand. It is Lord Warriner who is horrid."

"What have you to do with Lord Warriner?" asked Giles.

"Marriage!" said Arabella, tragically. "I know Lord Warriner is going to offer for me, and Mama wishes me to accept!"

"Lord Warriner?" said Giles in some surprise.

"He is so fat!" said Arabella. She began to sob again. "And so old. I care nothing for his money and his title. He pats my hand in such an odd way and calls me his pretty. Oh, Giles, he frightens me. And," she added, raising her head, "I love another who is young and handsome and writes poetry."

She buried her face in her handkerchief.

"Please, Arabella," said Giles desperately. "Please, do not cry. If you do not wish to marry Lord Warriner, then I'm certain you need not. These are not medieval times. No one can compel you to marry someone you do not like. If you love someone else who is suitable, I am certain that your parents will consent to such a match."

"But Mama says I must accept Lord Warriner," said Arabella, dabbing at her eyes.

"Why?" asked Giles.

"Because he is fabulously wealthy, and our fortune is not what it was. There are my sisters to be established. Mama is certain he will be most generous."

"I should think he would be," said Giles, checking himself as he spoke.

"I know they will never let me marry Jeremy," said Arabella.

"Jeremy?" asked Giles.

"Jeremy Tarkington," replied Arabella. "He is the one I love."

Oh, no, thought Giles. That will never do. Aloud, he said, noncommittally, "I will see what I can do."

"Please, Giles, you must help me," entreated Arabella. "I cannot marry Lord Warriner. If you do not help me, I don't know what I shall do!"

"You mustn't worry," replied Giles. "I am certain that you will not be forced to do something you do not wish to do. I promise you that."

"But what will you do?" asked Arabella.

"I don't know yet," replied Giles. "But I shall think of something."

"Thank you, oh, thank you," said Arabella, clinging to him. "I knew I could depend on you."

Giles disengaged himself quickly, promising to return when he had reached some solution. As he walked down the street, he began to see that he would have to deal carefully with the impulsive Miss Chedworth. Lord Warriner might not be an eligible *parti*, but neither was young Tarkington. He was still wet behind the ears. And a poet, no less. As if Byron were not enough! He would have to tread carefully. He would also have to be careful in how he approached the Chedworths.

It is certainly a good thing that my training is in diplomacy, he thought. Walsingham would be proud!

CHAPTER 16

In Mr. Stokes's office, things were not going well for Crippen, the clerk. Emboldened by a pint at lunch one day, he had indiscreetly revealed to Stokes's assistant how he'd put one over on Bradford when he'd tried to get information about Caroline Chessington. The assistant, appalled at this breach of a client's trust, had told Mr. Stokes, who had called the clerk in.

"You wanted to see me, Mr. Stokes?" asked the clerk.

"I hope that I have misunderstood what Mr. Potts has told me," said Stokes, with awful restraint. "Is it true that Adrian Bradford offered you money to reveal confidential information about one of our clients?"

Crippen looked from Stokes to Potts.

"Well, is it?" repeated Stokes.

"Yes, sir," said Crippen slowly.

"And is it true that you actually told Mr. Bradford about Miss Chessington's circumstances?"

"Well, sir . . ." He hesitated.

"Is it?" demanded Stokes. "Out with it!"

"Yes, sir," answered Crippen miserably.

"I cannot believe my ears," Stokes said, shaking his head. "That an employee of mine would violate the sacred trust that exists between a client and a man of business . . . and that client a lady! I am altogether shocked!"

"I'm sorry, sir," said Crippen, hanging his head.

"Sorry will not help, my lad, in these circumstances," Mr. Stokes replied. "I shall have to let you go."

"But, sir . . ."

"There is nothing else to be said," said Mr. Stokes. "I shall give you your wages for this week, but you must go." He stood up. Crippen opened his mouth as if to speak, but thought better of it and hurried out. Mr. Potts followed him.

Mr. Stokes sat back at his desk and examined his hands. Obviously, his responsibility dictated that he warn Miss Chessington, but it was a very delicate matter. Not only was he reticent about discussing such personal matters with his client; he also did not relish explaining to her how he had come by his knowledge. Mr. Stokes sighed. His duty, however disagreeable, was clear. He would have to call on Miss Chessington as soon as possible. He penned a note requesting the favor of a meeting and sent it with Potts, who returned with word that Miss Chessington would see him the following morning at eleven o'clock. Mr. Stokes was not looking forward to that meeting. No, indeed. He was not looking forward to it at all.

The next morning, Caroline awaited Mr. Stokes's arrival with a great deal of curiosity. The only other time he had requested a meeting with her was when she had come of age and assumed full control over her fortune. Then she had felt that he was easing his own mind, reassuring himself that she could handle it. Caroline smiled. How nervous he had been, how ill at ease! He was so unaccustomed to dealing with women, and he had been so nonplussed when she had asked him hard questions about her financial situation. Since then, with the exception of her visit to his office, their dealings had been through the post. Last week, he had sent a note indicating that he was still awaiting information on her request for money for Brampton, so he was not coming to see her about that. She could not imagine what he wanted.

When he was announced, Caroline was reading. She stood up and greeted him, requesting Briggs to bring some refreshments. They exchanged commonplaces for several minutes, and then

Caroline said bluntly, "There is something on your mind, Mr. Stokes. I wish you would tell me what it is."

Mr. Stokes cleared his throat. "It is my unfortunate duty to discharge a most unpleasant task," he said. "To think that such a thing could have happened in my office. I am only thankful that my honored father, in whose footsteps I followed, is not here to see it."

Totally bewildered, Caroline stared at Mr. Stokes.

"What can possibly be the matter?" she asked. "Has a clerk absconded with my funds? Am I now penniless?"

"Do not jest, Miss Chessington, I beg of you," said Stokes somberly. "This is no jesting matter."

"What is no jesting matter, Mr. Stokes?"

"I scarcely know where to begin," he replied. "You are . . . I believe . . . acquainted with Adrian Bradford."

"Adrian Bradford!" exclaimed Caroline. "What has he to do with this?"

"You met him, I believe, in my office," said Mr. Stokes.

"Yes, that's true," replied Caroline. "But I did not truly become acquainted with him until a chance meeting at the opera."

"I fear it was not chance that brought you together," said Mr. Stokes.

"Mr. Bradford did say that he had been hoping to see me again," said Caroline. "But I still do not see how this concerns you."

"I believe I betray no confidence if I tell you that Mr. Bradford, the scion of an ancient and honorable family, has lost most of his fortune through gaming and other—er—unsavory pursuits. It has saddened me to see his name sullied, for my connection with his family is a long one. I am aware that, for a long time, he has been seeking to contract a financially advantageous marriage to save him from ruin."

"But Mr. Bradford does not know that I am wealthy," replied Caroline.

"I regret to inform you that you are wrong," Mr. Stokes responded. "This is the aspect which so distresses me. One of my clerks—a man, I might add, who is no longer in my employ—was offered compensation if he would reveal information about you."

"What?" exclaimed Caroline. "I cannot believe it!"

"I am afraid it is true," replied Mr. Stokes dolefully. "You cannot imagine my feelings, Miss Chessington, on learning such news. It seems that Mr. Bradford is aware of your circumstances. He knows that you are a woman of large fortune."

For a moment Caroline stared at Mr. Stokes as if she were in a trance. Then, shaking her head slightly, she looked up at him and smiled.

"I can imagine how distressing this must be for you," said Caroline. "My family has always placed its trust in Stokes and Son, and we have never regretted it. I am certain that this was a great shock to you. However, there is no real damage done, and I hope we can continue as we always have done."

"Your graciousness is much appreciated, Miss Chessington," said Mr. Stokes, mopping his brow. "Had you known the trepidation with which I approached this meeting! You would have been justified in terminating your connection with my firm." He shuddered perceptibly at the thought.

"Nonsense," said Caroline briskly. "You refine too much upon the incident. After all," she said with a weak smile, "it is not as if I had married Mr. Bradford and he were now in control of my fortune."

"Do not think of such a terrible prospect!" replied Mr. Stokes. "I am only grateful that your acquaintance with him is slight."

At that moment, Briggs appeared with a tray.

"You will stay for some refreshment, Mr. Stokes," said Caroline.

"I must be going—well, perhaps a glass of Madeira would be welcome. I do not usually partake of spirits during the day, but this has been a most shocking experience."

Caroline continued to converse calmly, and soon Mr. Stokes was more relaxed. As he prepared to take his leave, he turned to her and said, "I cannot thank you enough for your kindness, Miss Chessington."

"Pray speak of it no more," said Caroline. "The matter is at an end."

Mr. Stokes bowed and left.

Caroline returned slowly to the parlor. Her thoughts were jumbled, one quickly following another. Her initial reaction to Stokes's disclosure had been shock, and she had responded to him mechanically, scarcely realizing what she was saying. What stayed in her mind and would not go away was the knowledge that Adrian had known from the first that she was an heiress. He had been truthful when he'd said that he'd sought her out, but it was not because he had been impressed with her. No, she had been purely incidental. It was her fortune he had sought, not her. He would not have approached her at the opera, would not have danced attendance on her at all if she had not been an heiress! She was hurt, but more than that, she was angry, as angry as she'd ever been.

"How dare he!" she exclaimed aloud. "How dare he make such a fool of me! And how stupid of me not to have realized. He gave me enough clues. His constant references to his financial situation, which I thought evidenced his frank and open nature, his fawning attention to Aurelia, which I thought so gallant of him. What a fool I've been!" She paced around the room. "Oh, when I see him, he is going to be very sorry. I will think of a plan to make him regret the day he ever met me in Mr. Stokes's office!" She sat down to compose herself by trying to think of a way to make Adrian Bradford pay for his perfidy.

And then the worst aspect of all hit her. Giles Kendal had warned her about Adrian Bradford, and she had sent him away. Now she would never see him again. And Giles had been right. That hurt more than anything. Not only had she been made a fool of by Adrian Bradford, but Giles Kendal would know that he had been right. Oh, it was unendurable!

CHAPTER 17

In the charming pink bedroom that Arabella had loved from the moment she'd first seen it, she sat sobbing on her bed. What she had feared had come to pass. Lord Warriner had approached her father, and Mr. Chedworth had given his blessing to the union. He had called Arabella in while Lord Warriner was still there and had told her of the great honor paid her. He had told her that the final decision rested with her, but Arabella knew this was not so.

That morning, Mrs. Chedworth had called Arabella in to see her. She had begun by admiring the flowers that Lord Warriner had sent. Then, she had asked Arabella if she were enjoying the Season.

"Oh, yes, Mama. Who would not?" she had replied.

"Indeed," said her mother. "You have had every opportunity a girl could desire. Gowns, bonnets, balls, and beaux. . . . What more could a girl wish for in her first Season?"

"Oh, nothing more, Mama," Arabella had answered. "I am very grateful for all that you and Papa have given me."

"You are a good girl, Arabella," said her mother.

"Thank you, Mama," replied Arabella.

"And you are no longer a child. That is why I am going to speak to you on a matter of importance and why I know your sense of responsibility will lead you to do just as you ought."

"Yes, Mama," said Arabella, this time barely audibly.

"You're aware, I am certain, of the growing attentiveness of one of your suitors. I need not mince words: it is Lord Warriner. I believe that he is about to approach your father."

"Oh, no," said Arabella involuntarily.

Mrs. Chedworth ignored the interruption. "There are many who would envy your position as Lady Warriner. In addition to consequence, a county seat, and a house in town, you would have a fleet of servants and one of the largest fortunes in England. While Lord Warriner is older than you, there are many successful alliances where such is the case. There is much to be said for an older, more settled husband."

"But I do not love him, Mama," said Arabella.

"Love often comes after marriage," said Mrs. Chedworth.

"Mama, I know things are not as they were, but we are not poor, are we? Must I marry for fortune and position?"

"My dear," said Mrs. Chedworth with a little laugh, "you must know that taking this house for the Season, your ball, and all of your gowns have cost a great deal! Your sisters must also be provided for, and there is the settlement to consider. You are a fortunate girl, and your papa has done what is proper. Now it is time for you to do your part. Your affections are not engaged elsewhere?"

"No, Mama," said Arabella untruthfully, feeling that she had no choice.

"At first I thought you had conceived a *tendre* for Jeremy Tarkington," said Mrs. Chedworth, "but I was correct in assuming that the infatuation would pass. If it had not, or if you had met someone else who was eligible, we would have dealt with that. As you have not, I think you know what you must do."

"Yes, Mama," replied Arabella.

"You do not dislike Lord Warriner?" asked Mrs. Chedworth.

"Mama," Arabella answered, avoiding the question, "Lord Warriner is not very handsome or young. And he looks at me so strangely."

"And I repeat, my dear," said Mrs. Chedworth, holding her impatience in check, "that Lord Warriner's age is not to be despised. An older man will pamper you. He will have his own interests and will not interfere in yours. I need not remind you, I am sure, that your pleasures must be handled discreetly. As for handsome, that is romantic foolishness which has no place in something as important as a marriage alliance. I know I can trust you. You have always been prettily behaved and done just as you ought."

"Thank you, Mama," said Arabella. "And may I go now? I have a letter I must finish to Susan Farnham."

"Certainly, my love," replied her mother. "And please tell Maria to lay out your pink muslin gown. You are looking a trifle pale, and you will want to look your best if Lord Warriner does call."

"Yes, Mama," said Arabella. She turned quickly and ran from the room.

That had been this morning. Lord Warriner had called, and she had appeared in the pink gown. She had accepted his offer, and he had not seemed to notice the trembling in her voice. Now she was back in her room and she could not seem to stop crying. But she had to! She had to think quickly. There was only one thing to do. She would have to run away. She could not marry Lord Warriner, but she could not tell Mama or Papa either. Papa would look unhappy, and Mama would call her an ungrateful girl. No, she would have to run away. Maybe she could become a governess. She could teach sketching; people had always admired her sketches. But how did one become a governess? And where could she go? She couldn't go home where she knew everyone, and anyway, none of Mama's friends would hire her. They'd be much more likely to send a messenger to Berkeley Square and she'd be carried back in disgrace. No, she would have to go someplace where she didn't know anyone. On the way to London, she remembered, there was a town called Bedford, where they had changed horses. There had been an inn, which had appeared quite respectable. Perhaps she could go there and stay until she found a suitable position. But she couldn't go without her maid—unless—unless she contrived a story. She could say that her maid had been taken by highwaymen. No, no one would believe that. But perhaps she could say that her maid had been taken ill on the journey. Yes, that would do. And she'd have to pack a bandbox after Maria went to sleep, so she could disappear before anyone awakened. Oh, there was so much to do! She wiped her eyes. There wasn't time for any more tears.

CHAPTER 18

When Adrian was announced the afternoon after Caroline's conversation with Mr. Stokes, she greeted him warmly. It seemed to Adrian that she was looking especially well. In fact, Caroline had taken special pains to look her best and was wearing a particularly flattering blue gown.

"Caroline, you look lovely," exclaimed Adrian, as he clasped her hand for a moment.

"Thank you," replied Caroline, smiling at him. "It seems that happiness agrees with me."

Adrian smiled in return. "It gives me pleasure to be the author of that happiness," he said.

Caroline blushed. "Indeed," she replied. "Little did I think, when I came to London for a brief stay, that I should come to think of London as home."

"Do you?" asked Adrian. "Do you truly feel at home here?"

"Yes, I do," Caroline answered.

"That relieves my mind of one worry," said Adrian. He took a turn around the room.

"What do you mean?" asked Caroline.

He did not answer immediately. When he did, he spoke slowly. "This situation is extremely difficult for me," he said. "I wish that you had a guardian—a protector—someone to whom I could speak about your future."

"There is Aurelia," said Caroline humorously.

"Do be serious, Caroline, I beg of you," said Adrian.

"But you are being absurd," replied Caroline. "I have no need for a guardian. I am of age. And it is not as if I had a large fortune or trust which would have to be settled," she added.

Adrian glanced at her quickly. "No, of course not," he said. "But, still, it would relieve my mind to know that someone with your interests at heart—shall we say—approved of my suit."

"But I do not need anyone's approval," said Caroline. "I know my own mind. I know that I shall not have wealth or estates, but we shall have each other. In fact, and I hope you will forgive my acting before you had declared yourself, I have taken steps to sell my property in Lancashire. We could not afford to maintain two establishments, and I know you will wish to remain in London."

"Sell Brampton?" exclaimed Adrian involuntarily.

"Why, you know of Brampton?" asked Caroline. "How can that be? I am certain I have never mentioned the name of my home."

"Ah, you forget, my dear, that you let slip the name on the day when we went to the Tower. And why should it be a secret?"

"I do not think I mentioned it," said Caroline.

"Well, perhaps Aurelia mentioned it," said Adrian. "You know how she chatters! Come, what difference does it make if I know the name of your home?"

"Because it makes me wonder what else you know about me," she said evenly.

"What else!" said Adrian playfully. "Have you deep, dark secrets you wish to hide?"

"I did," said Caroline, her voice tightening. "I came to London with a secret I wished to keep from everyone, but it appears that I did not succeed."

"Caroline, my dear, I have never heard you speak this way. Please tell me what has happened to distress you. You seem overset."

"I think it is time we stopped this charade," said Caroline. "I am aware that you have known, since the day I met you in Mr. Stokes's office, that I have a considerable fortune. I am aware that you sought me out because your circumstances made it necessary for you to marry a wealthy woman."

"You do not know what you are saying!" said Adrian.

"But I do," said Caroline. "I know that you have made a fool of me. I know that you would not be here now if you did not think me wealthy."

"That is not true," said Adrian, grasping at straws. "Perhaps it is true that I began my relationship with you because of your fortune, but if I had not been attracted to you I would not—could not—have continued it. And now I am here because I want to be. Because I love you!"

"Spare me at least this embarrassment," said Caroline. "Do not expose yourself further. I am furious at myself for having been so taken in, but the deception is at an end. I do not intend to reveal your character because to do so would be to reveal my own stupidity—but do not push me. You will leave this house and never come near me again. And now you will excuse me because I have nothing more to say." She swept out of the room, almost knocking down Aurelia as she rushed up the stairs.

"Caroline!" she called as she hurried downstairs to see what had occurred. As she entered the parlor, she was swept aside by Adrian rushing past.

"Mr. Bradford!" she exclaimed. "Pray tell me what has happened." Her only answer was the sound of the front door slamming. She looked around her, but the room provided no clue. "Well!" she exclaimed. "I do believe they have quarreled." She picked up her embroidery and began working on the cap she was making for a cousin's new baby.

For Adrian Bradford it was a time of desperation. He had been dodging his creditors for months and he was now at *point non plus*. Expecting at any moment to be able to announce his engagement to an heiress, he had been confident that, once again, he would escape Dun's territory. He could not believe that his scheme had failed! How had she discovered that he knew of her wealth? He had been so careful . . . and yet, somehow, she had discovered the truth. Was it Kendal? But how would he have known? Had Stokes gotten the truth out of that wretched clerk? In any event, there was nothing left for him to do but flee London. To stay was to court the public humiliation of bankruptcy and debtors' prison. Not even the Bradford name would save him this time. Once he was out of London, his creditors would have to find him . . . and he intended to make that difficult for them. Perhaps he would even go abroad, to France. Brummell himself had done that when his debts had grown too burdensome.

His first stop, before he could make any plans, however, would be at his sister's home in Northampton. He would try to play upon her fear of scandal to borrow passage money, at the very least. If luck were with him, her husband would not be at home. His brother-in-law would see that he would get not even a farthing from his sister. He'd made that clear the last time. But there was no one else. Yes, there was only one course open to him. He would leave London as soon as he could. Tomorrow would not be too soon.

CHAPTER 19

The note was delivered to Giles while he was still in his dressing gown eating breakfast. He was just finishing some excellent kippers when the butler came in.

"Excuse me, sir," said the butler. "There is a young person to see you. She says it is urgent, and that she comes from Miss Chedworth."

"Indeed!" exclaimed Giles. "Then I suppose I had better see her. Show her in."

"Very good, sir," said the butler. He returned shortly, followed by a heavily veiled young woman in a gray cloak.

"Please, sir, are you Mr. Giles Kendal?" she asked in a wispy voice.

"Yes, I am," said Giles. "And who are you?"

"I'm Maria, sir, maid to Miss Chedworth, and I have a note which she entrusted to me and told me to give to you no matter what happened to me." She clutched the note to her as she spoke.

"Please give me the note," said Giles, somewhat amused by the dramatics.

"Yes, sir," replied Maria as she handed the note to him.

Giles ripped it open.

Dear Giles,

I was not going to tell anyone of my plans, but I must confide in you, for only you can understand and help me. Lord Warriner has been accepted by my Papa and I am helpless to oppose. The only thing for me to do is to run away and become a governess. Then I can earn enough money to support Jeremy while he writes his poems. Maria is pledged to secrecy but Mama will surely come to you. Please tell her that I am well but that I cannot marry Lord Warriner.

I have taken my pearls (the ones Papa bought me for my come-out) and will have to sell them as I haven't any money except what is left from my allowance. As it is almost the end of the quarter, that isn't very much. I am certain I shall be all right and shall write to you (in secret) when I have found a situation.

Jeremy has no inkling of what has occurred. I am enclosing a separate note for you to give him. He will know what to do. I am depending on you both, for I am desperate.

Yours faithfully,
Arabella

"Good God!" exclaimed Giles when he had finished the letter. He turned to the maid. "Why did you not accompany your mistress?" he asked.

"Miss would not have me," she explained. "She said that governesses did not have maids."

"And you let her go?" asked Giles. "Did you not tell her mother?"

"Miss was being forced to do something she could not!" pronounced Maria dramatically. "It was my bounden duty to help her."

"You have a strange notion of duty," said Giles sternly. "But there is nothing to be gained in speaking of that. Have you no clues as to where your mistress may have gone? Did she say nothing?" As Maria hesitated, he said, "Come, I can be trusted."

"Well, sir, Miss did say she couldn't go anywhere where people knew her. I heard her wondering how much money it would take to get to Bedford."

"Bedford!" exclaimed Giles. "That's a day's journey from here. When did she leave?"

"Miss left before it was light," said Maria. "No one else is awake yet."

"That was three hours ago," said Giles, thinking aloud. "If she caught the early stage, she will have departed. I shall have to make inquiries at the station first and then follow on the road to Bedford."

"Please, sir, what shall I tell my mistress?" Maria looked frightened at the thought of the confrontation with Mrs. Chedworth.

"You shall take this note back with you." He penned a few words telling Mrs. Chedworth he was going to search for Arabella and would have word later. "If you are turned off, as I suspect you may be, come back here."

"Oh, thank you, sir," said Maria. She curtsied as she left.

Damn! thought Giles as he contemplated the note intended for Jeremy. He knew he should not open it, but propriety would have to give way to expediency. He opened the note and scanned it quickly. When he had finished it, he groaned.

"Good God, another Cheltenham tragedy!" he exclaimed. Arabella was clearly under the influence of some of the more fanciful novelists, but at least she had let fall some of her plans. Her first stop, it appeared, would be Bedford. At least, he thought, he had a direction. He wondered about delivering the note to Tarkington and decided reluctantly that bringing Arabella back to London would be more easily accomplished with him than without him.

Damn! thought Giles again as he contemplated the situation. But there was no time for that. He dressed quickly and within an hour was on his way.

Arabella had never before ridden in the stage. When she had come to London, it had been in her father's carriage, accompanied by her maid and surrounded by outriders. She had not shared it with other persons of the sort she was not at all accustomed to being with. The people she knew did not smell odiously, as that fat man did, or pinch her cheek, as that young man had. It had been difficult enough leaving the house without being observed. She had not wished to confide in anyone, but it had been necessary to seek Maria's help in packing a bandbox. Arabella had never packed anything in her life. She did not even know where her bandboxes were kept. Maria already knew the story of her persecution, so she confided in her the decision to flee. To Maria it sounded like a storybook: her pretty young mistress, in love with another, being forced to marry the rich old nobleman. Maria had pledged her silence. At the last minute Arabella had decided to send Giles a note. She was afraid to go without letting anyone know, and Giles seemed the right person. At least it eased her conscience about leaving her parents. She knew they'd be terribly worried. But it served them right. They had no right to force her to marry that fat old man!

With Maria's assistance, she had packed the bandbox by candlelight. It had been very hard to leave behind the pink silk with the florettes or the blue muslin which matched her eyes, but she wouldn't need them as a governess. Governesses didn't go to balls. A tear rolled down her cheek, but she brushed it away. From what she'd seen of governesses, they didn't cry, either. Governesses didn't do much at all, except teach Italian and sketching and get scolded when the children misbehaved. It was going to be very different from what she was used to, but much, much better than marrying Lord Warriner! With that thought she comforted herself.

There had been some difficulty about gaining a seat on the stage, the stationmaster taking exception to so young and obviously well bred a female traveling alone. But she had gazed up at him and told him of how her maid had been taken ill and how she was needed at home because her brothers and sisters had the measles and so she had to leave in the middle of the Season. It wasn't even such a very big lie, because they had had the measles. Whether the stationmaster believed her or not, he had shrugged his shoulders and taken the coins she offered. It never paid, he had discovered, to question the thinking of the Quality. Strange in their ways, they were. He had given Arabella a ticket and pointed to where she should wait. Then he had forgotten about her.

CHAPTER 20

It had been a very long evening. At dinner, Aurelia had tried to discover the source of the fight between Caroline and Adrian, only to be met by Caroline's discouraging, "I do not wish to speak of it, ma'am." There had been such a note of finality in her voice that even Aurelia had known better than to pursue the matter. Caroline had barely touched her dinner and had excused herself, saying she had the headache. As Aurelia well knew, Caroline was not subject to headaches or to any of the other ailments which troubled her own poor constitution, so this explanation boded ill. Aurelia made no attempt to follow her.

Caroline sat at her dressing table for a long while, looking at herself in the mirror.

"Well, my girl," she said aloud, "you've come full circle. When you decided to come to London you were sitting in your room, looking in the glass. As I recall, you were disappointed then, too, to discover that your most desirable feature was your fortune." She smiled weakly. "You know," she continued, "it's your pride, not your heart, that has suffered the worst hurt. You weren't really in love with him. You wanted to believe he loved you because he seemed to want you for yourself. You've been deceiving yourself, but now it's over." She put her chin in her hands.

"The thing is, what are you going to do now?" she asked herself after a few moments. "You can't leave London: it would show him you were running away." But suddenly the need to see Brampton, to go home, seemed overwhelming. "I don't care what he or anyone else thinks!" she declared. "I am going home!" She lifted her head defiantly.

"Sarah!" she called. Her maid came running to the door.

"Yes, Miss Caroline, what is it?" she asked anxiously.

"Sarah, we're going home to Brampton!"

"We are, miss?" asked Sarah. "But I thought . . ."

"Never mind that," said Caroline. "We are leaving in the morning."

"Tomorrow, Miss Caroline?" asked Sarah in surprise. "Will you be taking everything with you?"

"I shall take just a few things with me. In a few days I shall send you back with the carriage to collect the rest of my things and to help my cousin. I could not ask her to leave so quickly. Now, please send Briggs to me. I have arrangements to make."

"Now, Miss Caroline . . ."

"Please send Briggs to me," she repeated firmly. Sarah opened her mouth as if to say something, thought better of it, turned quickly, and left the room.

When the butler appeared at the door, Caroline said, "Briggs, I shall need the carriage in the morning."

Without blinking, Briggs said, "Indeed, miss. And may I ask at what hour you will require the carriage?"

"I should like to leave for Lancashire quite early—perhaps by eight."

"I beg your pardon, miss, but it may be difficult to make the proper arrangements for such a long journey with so little notice."

"I am certain it will not be difficult for you, Briggs," said Caroline with a smile. "I shall be leaving London, as I imagine you have surmised."

"It is not my place to question your intentions, miss," he replied firmly. "May I say, however, that I speak for all the staff when I say that we shall be sorry to see you leave us."

"Why, thank you, Briggs," said Caroline, touched by the comment.

"And now I shall see about the arrangements." He bowed and left.

"I suppose I had better tell Aurelia of the change in our plans," said Caroline. She smiled ruefully. "I have certainly left the hardest task for last."

She found Aurelia in her sitting room, reading sermons.

"Ah, my love," she said when Caroline entered. "I hope you are feeling more the thing?"

"Yes, I am," said Caroline. "But I find myself homesick for Brampton."

"That is quite natural," said Aurelia, "though you would not wish to leave our particular friends at this time."

"But that is exactly what I mean to do," said Caroline. "It is my intention to leave in the morning."

"The morning!" shrieked Aurelia. "But that is not possible! I could not possibly be ready!"

"You shan't be leaving tomorrow," said Caroline calmly. "I shall leave with Sarah. She will return in the carriage in several days to collect you and your possessions."

"But why?" asked Aurelia, fanning herself. "Why must we leave in this precipitous fashion? It is not at all dignified or proper. What of our engagements? The Waterloo Bridge opening . . ."

"I have decided that I wish to go home," said Caroline. "Our lease on the house is nearly up. Ah, and that reminds me that I must send a note to Stokes in the morning."

"Should you not inform our friends—Mr. Bradford, Mr. Kendal—that we are leaving?" asked Aurelia timidly.

"No," said Caroline. "I do not feel that is at all necessary."

"Please, my love, please tell me what has happened. Why did Mr. Bradford leave here so angry?"

"I do not intend to discuss the matter, Aurelia," said Caroline.

"And now if you will excuse me, there is much to do if I am to be ready in the morning." She turned and left the room.

"Oh dear," said Aurelia, shaking her head. "Oh dear, oh dear."

Caroline had asked to be awakened at sunrise, but she was already out of bed when Sarah came to rouse her.

"Up already, Miss Caroline?" scolded Sarah. "And you going to bed so late last night, insisting on writing letters and who knows what else."

"I fear I've been a trial to you lately, Sarah," said Caroline. "You quite sound like Mrs. Lawson, giving me a scold. I can just hear her."

"You're still not too old to scold, Miss Caroline," mimicked Sarah with a grin. "But you should put on your dressing gown and drink your chocolate. It's a damp morning, it is."

"Yes, ma'am," said Caroline meekly. "After I wash, I shall come downstairs for breakfast. Please tell Briggs I should like to see him then."

"Yes, Miss Caroline," said Sarah. "And mind you finish your chocolate!" She bustled out of the room.

"If I'm not careful, she'll soon be as bad as Mrs. Lawson!" said Caroline with a laugh. She finished her chocolate and began to dress.

While Caroline was eating breakfast, Briggs came in.

"You wished to see me, miss?" he asked.

"Yes," replied Caroline. "Is everything in readiness? I was not sure it could be done on such short notice."

"Of course, miss," said Briggs, his tone implying surprise at her doubt. "The carriage will be here at nine. Will that be satisfactory?"

"That is perfect," said Caroline.

"Briggs," continued Caroline, "I wish to thank you and the rest of the staff for your kindness during my stay in London."

"I am certain I speak for all the staff when I say that it has been our pleasure to serve you," said Briggs. "If your baggage is ready, I shall send the footman upstairs to bring it down."

"It is almost ready, I believe," said Caroline.

"Very good, miss," said Briggs. He bowed and left Caroline to finish her meal alone.

Caroline was upstairs when the carriage was announced. She quickly put on her hat and cloak and went downstairs. While Briggs supervised the loading of the bandboxes that she was taking with her, Caroline stopped to speak to the rest of the staff and to say good-bye to them.

Before leaving the house, Caroline handed Briggs two notes. Aurelia had not come downstairs, so Caroline had left a note for her. "I shall depend on you to see that Miss Peakirk receives one note and Mr. Stokes the other. I have printed Mr. Stokes's direction on the envelope."

"I shall see to it, miss," said Briggs.

"And please extend my apologies to Miss Peakirk," said Caroline. "I did not wish to disturb her this early in the morning."

"I understand, miss," said Briggs with a look that indicated that he did indeed.

Caroline entered the carriage, followed by Sarah. Briggs closed the door behind them. Caroline gave a final wave to the staff assembled in front of the house and they were on their way for the long drive to Lancashire.

CHAPTER 21

They reached Bedford in the early afternoon and stopped to change horses and have a light luncheon. As Caroline entered the inn the host came up to her, wiping his hands on his apron and bowing.

"Welcome to the White Hart, my lady," he said. "And what might you be wanting?"

"It is not my lady, it is miss," said Caroline with a smile. "And I should like a light luncheon. Is there a private parlor?"

"Well, yes and no," said the innkeeper.

"Yes and no?" said Caroline. "That is curious indeed."

"What I mean, my lady—miss—is that we have a private parlor but it is occupied at present."

"Then it is not available to me," said Caroline patiently. "We shall have to stop elsewhere."

"Oh, no," said the innkeeper, not at all anxious to lose custom of the sort which did not often come his way. "The room is occupied by a very young lady who came in alone. The missus, being a soft 'un, didn't want to leave her out here. I'm sure she wouldn't mind sharing the room."

"Very well," said Caroline. "Show me to the parlor and bring a light meal to me there."

"Right, miss," said the host. "If you'll just follow me this way . . ."

When they reached the parlor the host knocked on the door and opened it. The girl's back was to him as she looked out the window.

"Begging your pardon, miss, but here's a lady to share the parlor with you if you don't mind."

Caroline stepped forward. As she did the girl turned around.

"Miss Chedworth!" exclaimed Caroline. "What are you doing here?"

The girl, already pale, had turned white when she saw who stood in the doorway.

"Miss Chessington!" she bleated.

Caroline, conscious of the interested ears of the innkeeper, said, "What a delightful coincidence! As you can see, Miss Chedworth and I are quite old friends. If you will excuse us, we have much to catch up on." She nodded dismissal to him.

The host moved to the door reluctantly. "Will you still be wanting the food?" he asked.

"Yes, thank you," said Caroline. "Also, I think some ratafia would be welcome. Miss Chedworth appears a bit worn."

"Yes, miss," said the host. Caroline closed the door behind him.

"Miss Chedworth," she said when she was certain the innkeeper was out of hearing, "I know I have no claim over you, but I hope you will tell me what you are doing here unattended. If something is wrong I should like to help."

"Oh, Miss Chessington—" began Arabella. There was a knock on the door and the innkeeper entered with a tray on which there was cold meat, salad, two glasses of ratafia, and some fruit.

"Thank you," said Caroline, nodding dismissal.

"The missus says to please excuse the meal not being fancy-like as she 'adn't much time to prepare."

"It looks more than adequate," said Caroline. "Please thank her for me." This time the gesture of dismissal was more pronounced and the landlord took the hint.

"Please have something to eat, Miss Chedworth," said Caroline. She suspected that at least part of Arabella's tears were brought on by a lack of food.

"Oh, I couldn't eat anything," said Arabella.

"But you must," said Caroline. "If I eat alone I shall feel as if I am a pig. I am from the country and know that they are dirty creatures. I should not like to be one!"

In spite of her woes, Arabella giggled and took the plate Caroline handed her. For a few minutes she said nothing, for she was, in fact, hungry and had had to miss breakfast in her flight. When she had eaten all she could, she looked at Caroline expectantly.

"And now, Miss Chedworth, you must tell me how you come to be here," said Caroline.

"Please, Miss Chessington, call me Arabella," she said.

"And you may call me Caroline," said Caroline.

"Very well, Miss . . . Caroline," said Arabella. "I feel that you will be my friend—and I fear that I have no other." There was a sob in her voice as she finished the sentence.

"I am certain that is not true," said Caroline.

"But it is," said Arabella, "for I am being forced to marry Lord Warriner against my will and there is nothing anyone can do. Not even Giles Kendal can persuade my parents! That is why I have run away to become a governess until Jeremy and I can be together." She added defiantly, "I shall never go back to London!"

Her short time in London had acquainted Caroline with Lord Warriner by sight and she was surprised by Arabella's revelation.

"Lord Warriner!" she exclaimed. "I can quite understand your feelings. It would indeed be difficult to marry a man one finds so distasteful," declared Caroline.

"That is how I felt," said Arabella, "but I could not say so. Mama told me it was my duty because Lord Warriner is quite wealthy and my come-out has been so costly. When I marry, though, it will be for love and not wealth. I care nothing for wealth!"

"Is there some gentleman in particular for whom you have a *tendre?*" asked Caroline, trying to gauge the situation.

"Oh, yes," said Arabella, blushing. "I have met the most romantic man. He is so handsome and charming; all that Lord Warriner is not. And he is a poet, although as yet he is not appreciated as Lord Byron is, although he is much better. Mama says he is not at all suitable because he is a younger son and has no expectations. But that cannot be true. He is, after all, a Tarkington, the son of an earl."

"He sounds a veritable paragon," said Caroline dryly. "May one ask how old he is?"

"Jeremy is nineteen, almost twenty, but he is mature and wise. He is at Cambridge, you know. He agrees with me that love is more important in marriage than wealth," said Arabella.

"Does your mama know how you both feel?" asked Caroline.

"No. How could I tell her, when she went on and on about Lord Warriner and what an advantageous match it was. She does not suspect my true feelings," said Arabella tragically.

"Does Jeremy know that you have run away?"

"I wrote to him before I left."

Caroline thought for a moment as to the best way to dissuade Arabella from her present plan. She decided to convince Arabella to return with her to London. In the meantime, she would contact the Chedworths to let them know that Arabella was safe.

"Perhaps I can help you, Arabella," she said.

"But Caroline, what can you do? Mama will never listen. That is why I must become a governess. Mama will never think to look for me as a governess."

"I am certain you would not like the life of a governess," said Caroline. "From what I have seen, they lead very dull lives, and cannot marry, so you could not support Jeremy. It would not do for you at all. We shall have to think of something else."

Arabella, who had cheered during the discussion of Lord Warriner's shortcomings, sighed at Caroline's words. "I fear there is nothing to be done," said Arabella. "I told Giles—Mr. Kendal—what had happened and he said he would help me. But there was no time to wait for him."

"Then Mr. Kendal knows of your plans," said Caroline.

"I sent a note to him to be delivered this morning," said Arabella. "But I did not tell him where I was going."

"I am certain he will look for you," said Caroline.

"I will not return to London!" Arabella again proclaimed.

"You may stay with me until your parents have reconsidered," said Caroline soothingly. "I do not think you must begin your search for employment immediately. However," she repeated, "you should return with me to London so that we may discuss this with your parents."

"No, no, I will not return to London! They do not understand how I feel. If I return to London, all will be lost!" Arabella seemed about to succumb to a fit of hysteria.

Caroline reconsidered her plans quickly. "Then perhaps it will be better if you accompany me home. I am returning to Brampton."

"Brampton?" asked Arabella, her thoughts diverted.

"Brampton Hall," replied Caroline. "It is my home in Lancashire."

"You have a home in Lancashire?" asked Arabella. "But I did not think . . . that is . . ."

"You did not think of my circumstances," said Caroline with a laugh. "But I am quite an heiress. I inherited Brampton when my parents died."

"You did not seem so wealthy in London," said Arabella naïvely.

"No, I was hiding my wealth to see if I could find someone who would love me for myself. It did not work."

"I thought heiresses wanted everyone to know they were rich so people would want to marry them," said Arabella.

"Oh, many people wished to marry me," said Caroline. "At least they wished to marry my money and were willing to settle for me. I wanted something more."

"Did Giles know you were an heiress?" asked Arabella shyly.

"No, he did not," replied Caroline. "Mr. Kendal's friendship was genuine. But that is not helping us with your problem. I believe I shall send a letter to your parents, telling them that you are with me."

"Oh, no!" exclaimed Arabella.

"No matter how poorly you may feel that they have treated you, Arabella, I am certain they will be very worried if they have no word. I shall try to persuade them that if they continue to press Lord Warriner's suit on you that it will become known that your affections are engaged elsewhere. Neither your parents nor Lord Warriner would desire such a loveless match or such unfortunate publicity. I am certain Mr. Kendal would agree." She stood up and rang for the innkeeper.

"Have you some writing paper and a pen?" she asked when he appeared.

"Yes, miss, I'll get some right away."

While he was gone, Caroline turned to Arabella and asked, "Where is your baggage?"

"I have only one bandbox," she said. "I dared not take more with me."

"Of course not," said Caroline. "How foolish of me. Everyone knows governesses have no need of fancy clothes."

Arabella laughed. "Miss Chessington—Caroline—you do say the drollest things."

"I do remember my own governess scolding me for my shocking levity. Alas, I was hopeless!"

The innkeeper had returned with the writing utensils, which he placed on the table. Caroline sat down to compose a letter to Mrs. Chedworth. She wrote,

Dear Ma'am:

This is to inform you that Arabella is a guest in my house in Lancashire. I encountered her, unharmed, at an inn on the London Road, and felt it best that she come with me as she refused to return to London. She is apparently fearful that upon her return she will be forced into a marriage which she finds distasteful.

Whilst my position in this matter is rather irregular, may I suggest that your permitting Arabella to visit with me for a while will help avoid rumor and suspicion of a type which would be most unwelcome.

I may be reached at Brampton Hall, Lancashire.

I remain, respectfully,
Caroline Chessington

Caroline quickly reread the letter and sealed it. Then she penned a note to Giles Kendal, explaining the situation to him.

"I think we are ready to go, Arabella," she said. "The carriage must be ready."

They found Sarah already waiting at the carriage. Before entering it, Caroline handed the two notes to the innkeeper. "Please see that these are posted to London as soon as possible," she said.

"Right you are, miss," he replied.

"Sarah, this is Miss Chedworth, who will be returning to Brampton with us to visit."

"Yes, Miss Caroline," she replied, her lips pursed in evident disapproval of a young female traveling with a single bandbox and no maid.

"Miss Chedworth's maid inexcusably deserted her and she has been left stranded, Sarah. How fortunate that we stopped at this particular inn."

"Yes, Miss Caroline," said Sarah, apparently mollified and not wishing to annoy her mistress.

"I knew you would understand," said Caroline. As she settled first Arabella and then herself into the carriage, she paid no heed to the stage which had just arrived, nor to the traveler who was regarding them with interest. In fact, she did not see Adrian Bradford at all.

CHAPTER 22

When Giles arrived at the Tarkington residence he discovered Jeremy recovering from a slight indisposition. Upon reading Arabella's note and hearing Giles's plan for them to follow her and bring her back to London, Jeremy exclaimed, "Oh, my poor darling Arabella! Alone . . . unguarded . . . we must be off immediately. I will save her!"

"Good God!" exclaimed Giles. "Is that how you talk to her?"

"I love her," said Jeremy reverently. "She shall not marry Lord Warriner!"

"At last we agree," said Giles. "And now I believe we should—" He was not to finish the sentence.

"Mr. Kendal!" said Jeremy, interrupting. "Arabella will not return against her will. I shall see to that!"

"Careful, Tarkington," said Giles. "Remember, I stand your friend. I shall act in good faith. If Arabella will return, I shall endeavor to see that she is not forced to marry Lord Warriner."

"Sir!" exclaimed Jeremy. "You are truly—"

"If we do not leave soon," said Giles, interrupting in his turn, "Arabella may yet find a position as a governess."

They were soon on their way.

Giles Kendal and Jeremy Tarkington arrived in Bedford in midafternoon. Giles was familiar with an inn there, the White Hart, and decided to stop to ask if Arabella had been seen. When the host came out to greet him, he asked if Arabella had been there.

"I am looking for a girl, little more than a schoolgirl. I believe she is traveling alone, for her maid was taken ill. She is blonde and extremely pretty—and young. Naturally her parents are most concerned about her and have asked me to find her."

"Well, sir," said the innkeeper, rubbing his chin, "there was a female here as answers that description. Left here several hours ago with the other lady."

"The other lady?" asked Giles. "I am certain she is traveling alone."

"Well, she came alone on the stage," replied the innkeeper. "My missus put 'er in the private parlor, not wanting the young lady to mix with some of the rough 'uns. Then when the other lady came in asking for a private parlor, I showed 'er to the same one. Seemed like they knew each other."

Giles was completely baffled. "Do you know the other lady's name?" he asked.

The innkeeper rubbed his chin. "Well, sir, she said her name— it were something like Cherrington or Chessingham or something like that."

"Could it have been Chessington?" asked Giles slowly.

"Chessington," repeated the innkeeper. "I believe that was it."

"How on earth did she come to be here?" said Giles aloud. "Was she alone?" he asked the innkeeper.

"She come in a carriage and had a maid with her," was the reply.

"Where could she have been going?" asked Giles.

"I dunno that, but p'raps the letter would say," said the innkeeper.

"The letter?" asked Giles. "What letter?"

"The lady left two letters to be delivered to Lunnon on the next stage. Would you be wantin' to see 'em?"

"Yes, yes, I would," said Giles. "Bring them here, please."

"Yes, sir, right away." The innkeeper returned shortly with the letters and was suitably rewarded.

Giles examined the first address: Mrs. Chedworth. And it certainly was from Caroline Chessington. The second letter, to his surprise, was addressed to him. He opened it quickly.

Dear Mr. Kendal,

Whilst on my way to my home in Lancashire, I encountered Arabella Chedworth, traveling alone. She had run away to avoid a marriage to Lord Warriner and was determined to become a governess. I dissuaded her temporarily from that goal and persuaded her to accompany me to Brampton Hall. She was unwilling to return to London, so I saw no other alternative.

I have sent a letter to her mother explaining the situation and depend on you to convince her that forcing Arabella's return to marry Lord Warriner would be unfortunate.

I remain, yours sincerely,
Caroline Chessington

For a moment, Giles was too stunned to do anything but stare at the paper. He quickly reread the letter. Who did she think she was, interfering in matters that were no concern of hers! Unfortunate! Who is she to decide such matters? As if anyone would be interested in what Miss Chessington had to say. And what was this Brampton Hall? Pretty fancy for Miss Chessington, who took a house on Woburn Square.

The innkeeper cleared his throat and returned Giles to the present.

"Will there be anything else, sir?" he asked. "I have me work to do."

"No, nothing else," said Giles. "I need not open this letter." On the outside he penned a brief message: "Am following—G.K." and handed it back to the innkeeper. "Pray forward this as you were asked. And have my carriage readied. I shall be leaving at once."

"Right you are, sir," said the innkeeper. He saw no need to

mention that this was not the first request he'd had for information about the lady, nor that the other gentleman had left shortly after the ladies. There was no need to upset the Quality. So he said nothing, and in a short time, Giles and Jeremy were on their way.

CHAPTER 23

Several days later, when the Chessington carriage pulled up in front of Brampton, it was already dark and Arabella had fallen asleep, her head resting on Sarah's shoulder.

"Arabella, Arabella," said Caroline softly as she shook her gently, "we're at Brampton."

Arabella's eyes opened slowly and she looked at Caroline blankly, not remembering where she was or how she came to be there.

"It's Caroline Chessington," she reminded Arabella. "We're finally at my home in Lancashire. It's been a long trip. Are you awake now?"

"Oh, yes," said Arabella blearily. She shook her head.

"Sarah, please tell Preston that we have arrived."

"Yes, Miss Caroline," said Sarah.

"And tell Mrs. Sutton to prepare a bedroom for Miss Chedworth."

"I will, Miss Caroline," Sarah said wearily. She stepped out of the carriage. In a few minutes Preston came out.

"What a surprise, Miss Caroline," he said as he helped her out of the carriage. "We had no word of your arrival."

"My decision to travel was a sudden one. I hope I have not sent everyone into a frazzle!"

"No, indeed, Miss Caroline. I hope the staff know better than to slacken their diligence because you are not in residence. I have ordered the blue bedroom to be made ready for the young lady, and I believe the cook is preparing a light supper for you."

"Brampton could not exist without you," said Caroline. "Oh, how I have missed you all! How is Mrs. Lawson? I do hope her leg has quite mended! Now, I believe Miss Chedworth is quite done in and should be shown to her chamber."

"Very good, Miss Caroline," replied Preston. "I shall have your baggage brought in. I understand from Sarah that the rest is to follow with Miss Peakirk."

"Yes, that's right," said Caroline as she led Arabella into the house.

"How large it is!" exclaimed Arabella as she looked around her.

"It just seems that way because you have been confined in a small carriage for several days," teased Caroline. Mrs. Sutton came in then to take Arabella to her room, after first scolding Caroline for coming home so late.

"Take good care of her," said Caroline.

"Of course, Miss Caroline," replied the housekeeper with dignity. "I'm having a supper sent to her room."

"Thank you," said Arabella sleepily. She tried to stifle a yawn. She barely was aware of eating and being undressed before she fell asleep.

It was quite a bit later and Caroline was just starting up the stairs when the sound of horses was heard outside. She had just finished her own dinner and sent the servants to bed, so she went to the window to see who could be arriving at such an hour. To her horror, she saw Adrian Bradford approaching the house.

"Adrian Bradford!" she exclaimed. "How does he come to be here!" Not wishing to have him awaken the household with his arrival at such an hour, she ran to the door and opened it.

"I do not know how you come to be here, Mr. Bradford, but you are not welcome at Brampton!"

"It is a pleasure to see you, as well, my dear Caroline," said Bradford with an exaggerated bow. "However, the night air does have a chill and I wonder if we may continue this conversation inside."

"There is nothing to continue," said Caroline.

"My dear girl, if I were to arrive at the local inn at this hour with a story of being turned away from Brampton . . ."

"Your threats are nothing to me," said Caroline.

"Then do consider poor Arabella Chedworth," said Adrian. "Should I return to London, her escapade will scarcely escape notice. I shall make certain of that. What would London make of this melodrama?"

"What do you know of Arabella Chedworth?" asked Caroline sharply.

"I would prefer to discuss this inside," said Adrian.

"Very well," said Caroline reluctantly. "Come in." She led him inside and closed the door.

"Now, Mr. Bradford, what is it that you want? How did you know to come to Brampton and what do you know of Arabella Chedworth?"

"I must admit to a bit of luck," said Adrian, "although I would prefer to credit my skill. When I left London in some haste, to try to raise funds to leave England, I was fortunate enough to stop at an inn in Bedford. There I saw you and Miss Chedworth. I surmised, from your direction, that you were on the way to Brampton: a few coins were sufficient to elicit information from the innkeeper, a man of excellent hearing."

"So you still claim bribery as one of your talents," said Caroline.

"You have grown bitter," said Adrian. "You are not the charming young woman I knew in London."

"Indeed," said Caroline. "And what is it that you want from me now?"

"I wish sufficient funds to leave the country and set myself up in France. You are by far the plumpest pigeon I have to pluck."

"Impossible!" exclaimed Caroline. "I shall not yield to blackmail!"

"Then I shall be forced to return to London and to report this curious story to those most interested. Not merely the Chedworths, of course, but Lord Warriner and others who might concern themselves with Miss Chedworth's welfare. I am aware that you have written to the Chedworths to inform them of the situation, although delicacy prevented me from opening the letter. I would feel obligated to inform the rest of London."

"I have never met such a scoundrel as you!" exclaimed Caroline. "When I think that I encouraged your suit . . ."

"Had you accepted me, my dear Caroline, I would not now be forced to such actions which are so distasteful to me."

"You are beyond all bounds—" Caroline began, but she was interrupted again by the sound of horses. Both she and Adrian paused.

"Are you expecting more guests?" he asked. "I had no idea that Lancashire was so popular a destination."

"Certainly I am not expecting anyone," said Caroline through gritted teeth. "If you will excuse me, I shall see who it is. I do not wish the entire household awakened."

"Allow me to accompany you," said Adrian.

"I do not care what you do," said Caroline.

As Caroline walked to the door, Adrian peered through the window.

"What an odd time for Kendal to call," he commented. "And young Tarkington is most certainly *de trop*."

"Giles Kendal!" exclaimed Caroline. "What can he be doing here?"

"I suggest you open the door," said Adrian. He strolled up to her as Caroline let the visitors in. And it was he who greeted Giles.

"Welcome to Brampton," he said with a sneer.

As Adrian Bradford laughed and Jeremy Tarkington looked nervously about, Giles and Caroline stared at each other.

"I might have known," he said, breaking the silence.

"Known what?" demanded Caroline.

"Known that I'd find Bradford here."

"You could not possibly have known that," said Caroline angrily. "*I* did not know that he was coming here—any more than I knew that you were coming here. What are you doing here with Mr. Tarkington? Did you receive my letter? Have you spoken to the Chedworths? I do not understand how you come to be here now—and indeed, it was not necessary for you to come at all. I have the situation in hand."

"I can see that," said Giles.

"If I may interject a word," said Adrian, stepping forward. "In the first place, your voices are being raised. In the second place, I have no desire to interfere in what is clearly a private quarrel. Nor, I am persuaded, does young Tarkington. His feelings are of no consequence to me, but if you will assist me in my requirements, I shall take my leave. This house has become too crowded."

"What the devil is he talking about?" asked Giles.

"Mr. Bradford has come here to extort funds for passage to France as the price of his silence with regard to Arabella's flight," said Caroline.

"Succinctly put, my dear Caroline," said Adrian.

"Why, you—" said Giles, moving toward him. He was restrained by Caroline.

"Please, Mr. Kendal. We do not wish to awaken the household. Dearly as I should love to see him on the floor, I fear we shall have to accede to his demands. Far better to be rid of him."

"Yield to his blackmail?" asked Giles. "It is a matter of principle that one not yield to blackmail."

"Principle will be of little use to Arabella Chedworth if she faces social ruin because of a childish mistake."

"Arabella shall never suffer as long as I can defend her!" said Jeremy Tarkington, speaking for the first time. He flushed as they all regarded him.

"Bravo!" said Adrian.

"Mr. Tarkington," said Caroline. "If you will please wait in the morning room; it is the room to your left." Jeremy hesitated and then, confused as to his proper role in the situation, followed Caroline's instructions.

"Now," said Adrian when he was gone, "if we may return to the matter at hand . . ."

"Bradford—" said Giles menacingly, grabbing him by the lapels.

"Gentlemen," said Caroline, her voice dangerously calm. "I have had more than enough tonight. Mr. Kendal, I do not know why you are here; the situation was quite under control. Mr. Bradford, I wish you to leave at once. If the price of that be blackmail, so be it."

Giles began to speak, but Caroline forestalled him.

"Mr. Bradford, it is my earnest desire to be rid of you as quickly as possible. Whatever I have here, I shall give you. But beware. Should you return for more, or further exploit the situation, you will be most sorry. Mr. Kendal, I suggest that as soon as Mr. Bradford leaves—and I shall awaken one of the grooms, if necessary, to see that he does leave—you, Mr. Tarkington, and I retire for the night. All else can wait until morning."

Adrian bowed and Giles shrugged, saying, "As you will." He watched disapprovingly as Caroline finished her dealings with Adrian, and then closed the door behind him as Adrian vanished into the night.

When he had gone, Caroline turned to Giles.

"Mr. Kendal," she said, "despite my desire to retire immediately, I realize there are certain matters which must be settled. But," she added, her voice softening, "you look so tired. Let me offer you and Mr. Tarkington some refreshment."

"Thank you, we dined on the road," said Giles as he sat down wearily.

"Arabella's nerves are overset already. It would be unwise to tell her about Mr. Bradford's threats."

"Quite right," answered Giles. "And I shall warn Tarkington to be on his guard as well, although I don't know if he can be depended upon."

"What are we to tell Arabella about your presence here?" asked Caroline.

"I believe we should tell her the truth: that Tarkington and I both received her rather garbled notes, telling us that she had run away. Her maid mentioned the stage to Bedford. Inquiries at the stage office led us there and when we arrived in Bedford I discovered your notes. I read only the one addressed to me, I assure you. We followed you to Lancashire and several inquiries led us to Brampton. It seems you are well known in this region of the country, Miss Chessington, as a woman of parts."

"I am sorry I deceived you," said Caroline.

"You owe me no explanation," said Giles.

"Very well," said Caroline stiffly. "Let us discuss Arabella instead. Now that you are here, what shall we do?"

"It is my intention to take Arabella back with me tomorrow," said Giles. "Tarkington will be with us as well."

"Alone with both of you?" asked Caroline. "And without her maid?"

"May I ask if you have something better to suggest, Miss Chessington?" asked Giles a trifle impatiently.

"I will give it some thought. We can talk further tomorrow," answered Caroline. "Are you quite intent upon her returning home?"

"She belongs there, Miss Chessington."

"But Lord Warriner . . . the marriage . . ."

"Miss Chessington, Mr. Kendal, I will be heard!" said Jeremy, coming back into the room. "I will not be pushed aside! I will not be kept waiting any longer. If Arabella is to return to London, it shall be with me as her escort. As for Lord Warriner . . ."

"If Arabella is determined against the marriage, naturally she shall not be forced into it," said Giles. "I believe that can be arranged. A well-placed word in Lord Warriner's ear should do the trick there. I should have spoken to her parents earlier." Turning to Jeremy, he continued. "If, when you have both come of age, your feelings have not changed, I am certain the Chedworths would become reconciled to the match. They are not ogres, after all. I am sorry the matter got out of hand: one does not wish to interfere."

"No, of course not," said Caroline tartly. "Much better to let the child be bullied. You have been too long in the Diplomatic, Mr. Kendal. It has left you overly cautious."

Giles, worn out by his journey and goaded beyond thinking, exploded.

"I have heard quite enough from you," he shouted. "You dare to criticize my actions! You have misled Society about who you are—for what purpose one can only imagine! You have involved yourself with a man of unsavory reputation and refused to listen to warnings about him. You have involved yourself in the affairs of a virtual stranger. I come here to find you being blackmailed—but no more on that subject tonight! My conduct may be overly cautious, but your conduct is unspeakable! And now, if you please, I wish to retire. If you will be so good as to show me to a room . . ."

"With pleasure," she snapped.

When Arabella came down for breakfast the next morning, she found Caroline already there.

"Good morning," said Arabella. "I slept so soundly."

"Arabella, there is something I have to tell you. Last night, after you were asleep—"

"Good morning, Arabella," said a voice from behind. She whirled around to face Giles Kendal. Her hand flew to her mouth.

"Giles!" she shrieked. "What are you doing here? Does Mama know where I am? How did you find me?"

"Wait a minute!" said Giles, laughing. "I can only answer one question at a time."

"I must tell you, Giles," Arabella said seriously, "that I shall not return to London. I intend to find a position as a governess. I was on my way when Caroline—Miss Chessington—persuaded me to come here for a few days. I shall not marry Lord Warriner!" Her voice rose.

Exchanging a glance with Caroline, Giles interrupted her. "I believe we should return to London, but in the meanwhile, if you will permit me a word, I have other news for you which I am certain will please you. Miss Chessington has yet another guest, who arrived with me last night." Taking slight liberties with the truth, he added, "I tried to dissuade Mr. Tarkington, but he insisted on accompanying me. What do you say to that?"

Arabella squealed with delight. "Jeremy? Here? Where is he? When may I see him?"

Caroline laughed. "He seems to be still abed," she said dryly. "But I am certain he will arise soon enough. And now, Mr. Kendal, you were telling us your plan."

"As I started to say, we shall return to London immediately, for the sooner this is settled, the better. When we get to London I shall speak to your parents, Arabella, and to Lord Warriner, if that is necessary. I fancy there may be some slight difficulty, but I do not think either your parents or his lordship will press the issue. I am tolerably certain of that. For your part, let us have no more foolish talk of governesses, Arabella. I can imagine no one less suited for such a role! And now, if you will excuse me, Miss Chessington, it is time to waken Tarkington and begin to make preparations for our journey."

"Will you not have some breakfast first?" asked Caroline, hoping to avoid a retort from Arabella, who was looking mulish.

"Thank you, yes, although I do not wish to delay, as I know the Chedworths are very worried, despite your letter."

"I should like to speak to you before you leave," said Caroline. "Will you see me in the library before you go?"

Giles bowed. "Of course, Miss Chessington, I shall. But I must remind you that I have a long journey ahead."

"It will not take long," said Caroline.

"I will see you shortly," said Giles. He bowed again and left the room to awaken Jeremy.

"I am so happy!" said Arabella, pirouetting about the room. "I did not really wish to be a governess, even though Giles was mean to say that I wouldn't be a good one! Now I can hardly wait for Jeremy to awaken!" She stopped and looked at Caroline. "What have you to say to Giles?" she asked curiously.

"I have some commissions I wish him to execute for me in London," she said. "Do have some more to eat, Arabella, whilst you wait for Mr. Tarkington. If you will excuse me, I have some matters to attend to in the library."

After breakfast, Giles joined Caroline in the library.

"How may I be of service, Miss Chessington?" he asked.

"I would like to explain to you why I did not reveal my true situation to you or to anyone else," said Caroline.

"That is not necessary," said Giles. "Your personal life is your own concern."

"But it is important to me that I tell you," said Caroline. "Why must you be so stubborn?"

"I believe I am not alone in that trait," said Giles. "Pray continue, Miss Chessington."

"When I came to London, I had just refused another offer for my hand—"

"How boring that can be!" said Giles.

"Will you listen to me?" asked Caroline. "Another offer for my hand . . . and my fortune. I had received many offers, but none came from the heart. I was tired of being desired for my fortune alone, and so I decided to go to London as a mere 'Miss Chessington,' a provincial nobody of modest means. I did want to see London, and I wanted to see if there existed a man who could love me for myself."

"And so you found Adrian Bradford instead," said Giles sarcastically, "who turned out to be no better than a common blackmailer. How could you have succumbed to his threats and given him money? If you had not stopped me, I would have thrashed him and sent him packing!"

"I can see, Mr. Kendal, that you are not truly interested in what I have to say," said Caroline, her color rising. "You have decided to judge me on appearances, without consideration of the circumstances. It is a pity that you have not returned to diplomatic service. I fear that your long absence from diplomacy has robbed you of the ability to think rationally and speak tactfully."

"Have you quite finished, Miss Chessington?" asked Giles. He was very angry, the more so because he realized that he was in the wrong in not listening to Caroline's story. Matters between them, however, had gotten out of hand. It seemed that whatever he said sounded ungracious or petty, and yet he could not seem to make his words reflect his feelings, which had become clearer to him when he realized how distressed it had made him to find Bradford at Brampton.

"I have finished," said Caroline. "There is nothing more for me to say on this matter. I should like to turn to your plans for Arabella's return to London. She can scarcely be expected to travel back to London today after her arrival late yesterday. And she should not travel alone with you and Mr. Tarkington. Appearances aside, I strongly doubt whether either of you has the ability to keep her calm. Arabella is too high-strung to be without a suitable traveling companion and chaperone. I believe that we should return together. I am willing to accompany the party. It is true that it will delay the return to London, but I think it will be for the best." She did not admit to him, as she was forced to admit to herself, that she did not want him to leave, perhaps for the last time.

"Perhaps you are right," said Giles. He realized with a pang that he did not want to part from Caroline Chessington while things were still so disagreeable between them.

"And Mr. Kendal," said Caroline.

"Yes, Miss Chessington?"

"It will be a long and difficult journey back to London. I trust that we can both be depended upon to set an example for our charges. Our personal feelings should not be permitted to intrude on our responsibilities."

"I quite agree," said Giles, nettled again. "There is no reason for our personal difficulties to affect the discharge of our duties. Your opinion of me to the contrary, my professional training has indeed prepared me to carry on regardless of the unfortunate circumstances."

"Are you regarding me as an unfortunate circumstance?" asked Caroline, her eyes flashing.

"Certainly not," said Giles. "It is the necessity of my continued involvement with you which is the unfortunate circumstance. And now if you will excuse me, Miss Chessington . . ." He turned and left the room, the door receiving an unnecessarily hard pull as it closed behind him.

"Again!" said Caroline through gritted teeth. "Again that insufferable man has had the last word!"

CHAPTER 24

The journey to London was not a happy one. Arabella would not enter a carriage without Jeremy by her side, so Caroline, in her role as chaperone, found herself crowded into a carriage with a silly widgeon who wavered between despair and joy, and a foolish halfling who bravely offered to call Lord Warriner out if that gentleman approached his beloved. It was trying enough to cause Caroline to wish she were in Giles Kendal's carriage, but as the thought of Giles was quickly accompanied by similarly unsettling feelings, she brushed aside such thoughts and applied herself to controlling her companions.

They stopped for meals and lodging at inns along the road. At each stop Giles reserved a private parlor and the best rooms for their use. He was feeling considerably ashamed of himself for his outburst at Brampton. He bitterly regretted that he, a trained diplomat, had succumbed to such pettiness. It was, he reflected moodily, time he returned to Vienna. In retrospect, it was evident that Caroline Chessington had only been trying to help; that, in fact, she had very probably averted a scandal. But he found it difficult to speak to her, to tell her how he felt, for she refused to leave Arabella and Jeremy alone and her reserved demeanor and coolness when he spoke to her did not make him feel that she had forgiven him.

Before leaving Brampton, he and Caroline had agreed to stop in Woburn Square and leave the two lovers under her chaperonage while Giles went to see the Chedworths. For Caroline it was an awkward entry into London. She had left under uncomfortable circumstances and was not looking forward to explaining that situation to Aurelia. And then there was Giles Kendal to deal with. She had avoided him so successfully on the journey to London that it was possible that she had discouraged any further attempts to renew their friendship. Now, removed by time and distance from their quarrel, she was not at all certain that she wished Giles Kendal out of her life.

It was true that he had made her very angry, but now that her good temper was restored she reflected on how solicitous of her comfort he had been on the journey, reserving private parlors and ordering special meals. It had not been easy, finding suitable accommodations on short notice for such a party, and much persuasion had been required, as well as money changing hands. Caroline had noticed at their last stop that Giles looked drawn and tired; for someone still not completely restored to health he had overexerted himself—perhaps even risked permanent harm—to save Arabella Chedworth's reputation. Then she shook off these thoughts. As things stood between them, it was foolish to think of Giles Kendal any more than she had to.

It was a surprised Briggs who answered the door and greeted the returning party in Woburn Square, but he quickly regained his aplomb.

"Welcome home, Miss Chessington," he said, helping her out of the carriage.

"Thank you, Briggs," she replied. "I realize this is most sudden and I am afraid I have caught the staff unawares."

"The staff, Miss Chessington," said Briggs with dignity, "is always prepared. Miss Peakirk is still in residence."

"Of course," said Caroline. "And is she at home now?"

"Miss Peakirk has gone out," said Briggs.

Caroline breathed a sigh of relief. "Then please show Miss Chedworth and Mr. Tarkington into the morning room," she said.

"Very good, miss," said Briggs. "And I shall have a light repast sent in."

"Thank you, Briggs." She turned to Arabella, who was looking frightened.

"Do go with Briggs," she said. "I shall be in presently and he will make you comfortable."

Arabella followed, but Jeremy lingered behind.

"I believe . . . that is, it is my duty . . ." he began, but Caroline interrupted him.

"Mr. Tarkington, I must entrust to you the care of Miss Chedworth. She is very apprehensive and I am relying on you to reassure her. We do not wish her to work herself into a hysteria. Do go to her."

Thus appealed to, Jeremy followed Arabella inside. Just then Giles's carriage, which had been behind them, pulled up in front of the house. Caroline waited to greet him.

"Welcome to Woburn Square," said Caroline as he descended from the carriage.

"Are you pleased to be back in London, Miss Chessington?" he asked.

"My return here, Mr. Kendal, was purely a matter of necessity. I shall not remain longer than is required."

"I trust this matter shall be resolved shortly," said Giles. "I stopped here to tell you that it is my intention to go to the Chedworths' immediately. The sooner this affair is at an end, the sooner I can make plans for my return to Vienna."

"Will you be returning soon?" asked Caroline.

"As soon as the doctor says I may," said Giles. "After traveling the length of the country, a mere trip to Vienna should not be too arduous."

"I think I should be going inside," said Caroline, her voice carefully expressionless. "I must see to my guests."

"I shall return as soon as I can," said Giles. He bowed, and as their eyes met, he said simply, "Good day, Miss Chessington!"

"Good day, Mr. Kendal," said Caroline. She turned and went inside.

Briggs had set out a lovely meal, to which Jeremy was doing justice. Love, thought Caroline wryly, had not affected his stomach. Arabella, however, was picking at her food. She constantly shifted her gaze to the door as if she expected her papa to walk in at any moment.

Caroline was entreating Arabella to try some cold meat when the door opened and Aurelia burst in. She gave a little shriek when she saw Caroline.

"When Briggs told me you were here, Caroline, I could scarcely credit it! I thought you were at Brampton! How come you to be here again? Caroline, you cannot mean to continue in this helter-skelter manner. It is not at all the thing. I declare, I am nearly distracted!" She pulled out her vinaigrette.

"Dear Aurelia," said Caroline. "I know you have sustained a shock. Pray come with me so that I may explain to you what has happened." She was eager to remove Aurelia before she noticed Arabella and Jeremy and before her heedless remarks could set Arabella off again. Caroline put her arm around Aurelia and led her into the library. Briggs, who had been lingering near the door, followed with two glasses of ratafia and exited wordlessly.

"Now Aurelia," said Caroline, firmly sitting her down and handing her a glass. "Let me explain."

"Oh, Caroline," said Aurelia, dabbing at her eyes. "I do not understand what is happening. Things used to be so comfortable. You never used to do such unexpected things. Leaving town suddenly, with no explanation . . . and then reappearing, just as I was preparing to leave for Brampton. Oh, I begin to wish we had never come to London!"

Caroline forbore reminding Aurelia that she had always urged Caroline to visit London and had been delighted when she'd learned of the planned trip.

"And why is Arabella Chedworth here?" Aurelia asked querulously. "How came she to be in your company? And who is that gentleman?"

"Arabella is with me while Giles Kendal speaks to her parents," said Caroline.

"Giles Kendal!" exclaimed Aurelia. "I do not understand what he has to do with this. Do tell me that there will not be a terrible scandal and that we will not be ruined! We must return to Brampton and stay there. Perhaps all will be forgotten before I die!"

"Pray calm yourself, Aurelia," said Caroline with a laugh. "You take too dismal a view of the situation. There will be no scandal. Mr. Kendal will explain to the Chedworths why Arabella does not wish to marry Lord Warriner. I have no doubt that they will accede. Mr. Kendal will see to that! The betrothal will be terminated—not such a rare occurrence, you know!—and all will be forgotten as soon as something more interesting occurs."

"I do not understand you, Caroline," said Aurelia weakly. "First you reject Adrian Bradford, who was such a gentleman. Then you leave London and return with Giles Kendal! Perhaps," she said, her eyes brightening, "you are going to marry him?"

"Certainly not," said Caroline sharply. "I do not intend to marry Giles Kendal and I am certain he does not intend to marry me."

"Oh, dear," said Aurelia, dabbing at her eyes, "it would be such a good thing if you did. Then you would not go pelting about the country."

"No," said Caroline, laughing. "I would be in Vienna, so I could scarcely pelt about the country. But I would be far from Brampton and you, and I should not like that." She kissed her cousin. "No, I should not like that at all."

CHAPTER 25

When Giles was announced at the Chedworths', he fortunately found them both at home. Mrs. Chedworth jumped up and ran to him as he came into the room.

"Have you found Arabella?" she demanded. "What is all this about? Where is Arabella? Is there to be a scandal? I have received the oddest note from Caroline Chessington, whom I scarcely know. I demand to know what has happened!"

"Arabella is quite safe, ma'am," said Giles. "And no, a scandal has been averted, thanks to Caroline Chessington."

"I am certain I do not understand her involvement in all this," said Mrs. Chedworth. "I should never have invited a female of whom I know nothing to Arabella's ball. I hold you responsible for that, Giles. Her racketing about the country and interfering in the lives of her betters is proof of her lack of respectability."

"It would be wise if you did not criticize Miss Chessington," said Giles. "She has saved you a great deal of unpleasantness and you are greatly in her debt. As for her respectability, her birth is quite as good as your own."

"Indeed!" Mrs. Chedworth tittered. "How fortunate she is to have such a champion. Are we to wish you well?"

"Miss Chessington does not need a champion," said Giles. "She is," he added with a rueful smile, "quite capable of taking care of herself."

"Come, Kendal," said Mr. Chedworth, joining in the discussion. "Where is Arabella?"

"Arabella is with Miss Chessington in Woburn Square," said Giles.

"Miss Chessington, Miss Chessington! I still do not understand how she comes to play such a role in this? And why did not Arabella return home with you? Until she does, we cannot tell Lord Warriner that all is well," said Mrs. Chedworth. "It has become very difficult to explain to him Arabella's absence. He knows there is no indisposition and I believe he may suspect that she has, in fact, run away."

"It is of Lord Warriner that I wish to speak," said Giles. "Of Lord Warriner and Arabella. Arabella does not wish to marry Lord Warriner. In fact, she holds him in such aversion that I believe she should be released from her engagement. An engagement, I might add, which I believe to have been ill-advised. To affiance a young, inexperienced girl to such a—"

"You overstep the bounds, Kendal," interrupted Mr. Chedworth angrily.

"Indeed, Giles," said Mrs. Chedworth, "I believe we must be the best judges of such matters. Since you do not intend to offer for Arabella, it is not your concern if someone else has."

"It is indeed my concern," said Giles. "I have just spent a trying week pelting about the country in pursuit of Arabella—to prevent, I might add, the sort of scandal of which you are most afraid. I believe that gives me a direct interest in this matter. I have given Arabella my word that she will not have to marry Lord Warriner. It was only with that promise that she would agree to return."

"Arabella will do as she is told," said Mrs. Chedworth. "I have had quite enough."

"If," said Giles in measured tones, "you continue to insist that Arabella marry Lord Warriner, her distaste for the match will be made known. I do not think Lord Warriner should care for that, nor will it reflect well on you. If Arabella should go into a decline, you will bear Society's censure."

"You cannot do that," said Mrs. Chedworth. "You, the son of an old and dear friend! You cannot mean to do that!"

"I can and I will," said Giles. "I am exceedingly tired of this entire episode. Were it not for your folly, it need not have occurred at all. Now I have a solution. Arabella has taken it into her head that she wishes to marry Jeremy Tarkington. His birth is unexceptionable and his prospects respectable; while he may fancy himself a poet, with proper direction, we need not despair of him. I urge you to permit him to pay his addresses. The romance may not stand the test of time, but if it does, it would be wise to allow the marriage. Arabella has run away once. This time there were no ill effects. You may not be as fortunate again."

Mrs. Chedworth regarded her husband, who did not speak for several moments.

"I do not see that we have a choice," he said finally. "A scandal will merely result in Arabella finding herself an outcast from Society. It would then be impossible to arrange any favorable alliance. We shall have to end the betrothal and trust in Lord Warriner's—and your—discretion. As to the poet . . ." He grimaced.

"If you wish your daughter's return," said Giles, "if you hold her in affection—and I know you do—"

"We shall have to permit Tarkington entrée," said Mrs. Chedworth. "It is not what I would like, but it is our only choice. Perhaps it will not last."

"Splendid!" said Giles. "Then I shall tell Arabella that she may return home safely. In fact, I shall return to Woburn Square and see that she returns immediately. I must warn you, however, that she will not travel without Tarkington."

"We shall have to welcome him sometime," said Mr. Chedworth.

"You have made a wise decision," said Giles. He took Mrs. Chedworth's hand. "I know you are not well pleased with me now, but I am certain it will be for the best." With a bow, he was gone.

"I know that ruin stares us in the face," said Mrs. Chedworth. "If only they had not interfered!"

"On the contrary," said Mr. Chedworth. "Far from hastening our ruin, they may have saved us!"

When Giles returned to Woburn Square he found Arabella, alarmed by his prolonged absence, in a state that even Caroline's common-sense talk and Jeremy's devotion had been unable to avert. When she saw him she ran and threw her arms around his neck.

"Oh, Giles, have you seen them?" she cried. "What did they say? I know it is something terrible and Jeremy and I will be forced to flee."

"Arabella, calm down," said Giles firmly, extricating himself from her grasp. "It is past time that you ceased enacting these Cheltenham tragedies. You are too much in alt. Come, Tarkington, you will have to do better at dealing with Arabella if you are to persuade the Chedworths of your value!"

"Then there is a chance, Giles?" asked Arabella.

"Your parents have agreed to terminate your betrothal to Lord Warriner," said Giles.

"Oh, Jeremy!" said Arabella, flinging herself this time into his arms.

"Then they have agreed with our point of view?" asked Caroline.

"They have agreed that forcing Arabella to marry against her will is unwise and, as they do love her, unfair."

"And what of Jeremy?" asked Arabella. "Do they know that I mean to marry him?"

"They have agreed to permit him to pay his addresses. If the relationship lasts, they will countenance a betrothal."

"But I consider myself betrothed to Jeremy now!" said Arabella.

"Surely you can wait a little while," said Caroline.

"Jeremy and I do not wish to wait!" said Arabella. Everyone turned to Jeremy, who blushed.

"Have to wait," he replied, looking at his beloved. "I don't come into my income until next year," he explained, taking his new responsibilities seriously.

"A sensible plan," said Caroline approvingly.

"Oh, Jeremy," said Arabella, beginning to cry. "I'll wait for you. I'll wait for you forever."

"I believe," said Giles, "that this lamentable affair is finally at an end."

CHAPTER 26

When a tearful Arabella, accompanied by her Jeremy, was safely on her way to Berkeley Square, Giles and Caroline turned to each other. Without quite realizing it, they had gone through the last several days happy with the knowledge that they would see each other again. Now the adventure was over and there was no further reason to continue their acquaintance. Giles knew he should take his leave. He knew he should bid Miss Chessington good-bye, put Miss Chessington out of his mind, and direct his thoughts toward returning to Vienna. There was no reason to stay. Yet he stood, unwilling to go.

Caroline knew that she should indicate to Mr. Kendal that their acquaintance was at an end. She knew that she should graciously extend her hand, thank Mr. Kendal for his kindnesses during their journey, and see him to the door. Yet she, too, stood, unwilling to say a final good-bye.

At last she spoke.

"Mr. Kendal," she said, holding out her hand.

"Yes, Miss Chessington?" he asked, taking it.

"I should be reluctant to part without thanking you for your kindness to me these last few difficult days."

"I was pleased to be able to serve you," said Giles.

"As you will be returning to Vienna, perhaps I shall not see you again. I should hate to part with ill feelings between us."

"As should I," said Giles. "It would be a most unfortunate circumstance." They both smiled at the memory of those words, and then remained standing there a bit awkwardly. Again, Caroline broke the silence.

"Mr. Kendal," she began again, "at Brampton I tried to explain why I came to London incognita. I should like to finish that explanation before you go."

"My behavior in refusing to listen was quite childish and ill-mannered," said Giles. "It was conduct not befitting a member of Lord Walsingham's staff!"

Caroline blushed as her words, too, were recalled.

"I told you that I came to London to see if there existed a man who could love me for myself and that I found instead Adrian Bradford. I did not know at first that he knew of my wealth. I did not know until shortly before I left London, when my man of business told me that Adrian Bradford had bribed a clerk to discover my identity. Imagine my humiliation! I had known, deep down, that he was insincere, but I wanted to believe that he loved me and, until the end, I had no reason to think he was deceiving me."

"I did not know this," said Giles slowly. "I can understand now how you could have wanted to believe that Bradford was genuine."

"Yes," said Caroline. "You cannot know how pleasant it was to hear the sweet words he spoke and to feel the warmth he showed. At first, after our initial meeting, I thought your interest was piqued, but then it seemed to wane. That is when I turned to Adrian Bradford."

Giles smiled ruefully.

"The more you turned to Bradford—a man I despised—the more disturbed I became and the more I wanted to warn you away from him. I thought you incredibly stubborn and foolish to be so taken with such a scoundrel."

"I did want to believe in him," said Caroline. "So much so that my common sense was suspended."

"Then my warnings to you were most unwelcome," said Giles.

"More than unwelcome," said Caroline. "You were merely confirming what I felt to be true and did not want to believe. And at the same time you seemed to be making a fool of yourself over a child just out of the schoolroom!"

"What the devil are you talking about?" demanded Giles.

"You seemed so charmed by Arabella. You had a kind of fatuous smile . . ."

"Have you lost your reason?" asked Giles. "Arabella?"

"Tell me that you were not infatuated with her," said Caroline.

Giles took a deep breath. "I suppose I was for a time," he admitted. "She was so young and innocent . . . but, my God, Caroline, I soon discovered she's a mere child! Artless, charming —for about an hour. I began to fear I'd said too much and might be forced to offer for her. Luckily for me, her mama would have none of an earl's younger son."

"And that's another thing," interrupted Caroline. "You didn't tell me you were the son of an earl."

"I guess I, too, just wished to be liked for myself," he said. "I'd been ill, I was tired and worn out, and I didn't want still another female fawning over me."

"What a terrible problem," said Caroline. She laughed, and Giles did, too.

There was a pause in the conversation. Both seemed about to speak, but neither knew what to say. For the third time, Caroline broke the silence.

"I know we must say good-bye," she said, "although I feel we still have much to say to each other." She turned away and walked toward the window, fearing she had said too much.

Giles followed her and put his hands on her shoulders, turning her slowly around until she faced him.

"Why must we say good-bye?" he asked. "You are right, there is still much we have to say, much that I have wanted to say these many days, but each time I tried, we ended up at sword's-point. I have wanted to tell you how much I admire you; how I have felt drawn to you from the beginning. Do you recollect, at Arabella's come-out, when we were standing on the terrace? Then Bradford appeared and you went off to dance with him. I was so jealous, and I behaved so foolishly!"

"I could not imagine why you became so cold and distant," said Caroline.

"I could not bear to see you beguiled by Adrian Bradford," said Giles. "When I thought I had lost you to him I could not believe it. I realized then how much I cared for you. Oh, how I envied him! Caroline, say there is still time for me to say those sweet words that you desire to hear and that I long to say."

"There is all the time in the world," said Caroline breathlessly.

Giles drew her closer to him, his arms embracing her tightly. He looked down at her upturned face, her lips soft and inviting, and slowly his lips met hers, first gently and then more demandingly. Caroline's hands caressed him as she returned his kisses hungrily.

Later, when they were seated on the sofa, Giles said softly, "Now I can tell you how much I love you. And that I loved you before I knew you were a woman of wealth and substance, and thought you only a woman of charm and wit. Will you marry me, Caroline, even though I am the son of an earl?"

"But only the younger son," Caroline reminded him as she moved closer into his arms.